A DEMON'S Wrath

PEACHVILLE HIGH DEMONS
PART 1 & 2

SARRA CANNON

A Demon's Wrath
Copyright © 2013 by Sarra Cannon

All rights reserved. This book or any portion thereof
may not be reproduced or used in any manner whatsoever without the
express written permission of the publisher except for the use of brief
quotations in a book review.

Printed in the United States of America.

Cover Design by Robin Ludwig Design, Inc.
Editing Services by Janet Bessey at Dragonfly Editing
Formatting by Inkstain Interior Book Designing
www.InkstainFormatting.com

BOOKS BY SARRA CANNON:

YOUNG ADULT

PEACHVILLE HIGH DEMONS SERIES:

Beautiful Demons
Inner Demons
Bitter Demons
Shadow Demons
Rival Demons
Demons Forever

A Demon's Wrath: Part 1
A Demon's Wrath: Part 2

ETERNAL SORROWS SERIES:

Death's Awakening
Sorrow's Gift

NEW ADULT

FAIRHOPE SERIES:

The Trouble With Goodbye
The Moment We Began
A Season For Hope
The Fear Of Letting Go

Sacrifice Me

—To all the loyal fans of the
Peachville High Demons series.
You have made my dreams come true.

PART I

TWO STONES
OCTOBER 31, PRESENT DAY

*I*N MY LIFETIME I have been known by many names.

Denaer. The name my mother and father chose for me on the day I was born. In the world of my ancestors, this name meant favored one. Blessed because I was a twin. A shared soul—something very rare and powerful among my kind.

Wrath. The name the witches of the Peachville coven gave me when, in my rage and my sorrow, I slaughtered so many and forced my way into their world.

Jackson. My human name. The only name I chose for myself. In this world, the name means God has shown favor. It was the closest I could find to my demon name and at the time, I thought it was ironic that one such as I could be considered blessed after all I'd done and all I'd lost.

But tonight, on Halloween, the anniversary of the day my brother was taken from the demon world and brought here to be a slave, I knew that I was blessed.

Below, the sound of laughter and music carried up the stairs and into my bedroom.

It was the laughter of those I loved most, safe and free after all this time.

I smiled and pulled my shirt on, my hands trembling slightly as I buttoned each of the small buttons. I straightened my arms, then closed and opened my fists, but they were slightly numb. And sweaty.

I wiped my palms against my black pants and took a deep breath in and out.

Tonight would be one I would never forget, and I wanted it to be perfect.

Two stones weighed heavily in my pocket and every time I moved or took a step, I felt them brush against my leg.

One was a memory stone made of quartz.

The other was a smaller stone locked inside a golden case.

Closing my eyes, I took another deep breath. In order to move toward my future, I knew I would have to face my past. If Harper was to ever really understand me, she would have to also understand my greatest triumphs and my darkest secrets.

I walked to the window and looked down. This was where she had been standing when I first saw her. Our eyes met and there was an instant connection. Something neither of us fully understood at the time, but would change us both forever.

I reached my hand inside my pocket and closed my hand around the cool quartz.

I searched my memory, trying to decide where it all began. Where my story should start. Then, I let the images of my past flow through me and into the magic of the stone where they would be locked inside for Harper to see.

HOW COULD I HAVE BEEN SO BLIND?
THE SHADOW WORLD

*T*HE FLAME BARELY missed my head as it sailed past. My eyes widened. "Careful," I said, scowling at my brother, Aerden. "You almost hit me with that one."

He raised an eyebrow. "I can't help it if you're too slow."

Fine. If he wanted to play rough, I'd give him rough.

I lifted my hand toward the stream that ran beside us. A long, thin rope of water rose up, curling into a circle on one end. I thrust my hand forward and the rope sailed through the air, then slipped over Aerden's head. I pulled back, tightening the rope around his neck.

But before I could turn the water into ice, he shifted into a swirling mass of black smoke.

The water lost its form and splashed against the black rock below.

Crap. I was never fast enough.

I followed Aerden's trail, but miscalculated and realized my mistake too late. Misdirection was one of his many strengths in battle and today especially, I was finding it hard to keep up.

The sharp edge of his axe pressed against the back of my neck. I tried to shift, but I was too late. Pain held me to my solid form.

Aerden laughed, but it wasn't a happy sound. He was tense and angry, and I couldn't make sense of it.

"What's gotten into you today?" I asked when he finally removed the blade from my neck.

He shrugged. "I don't know what you mean," he said. "We're just sparring. It's not like I was really going to hurt you."

I rubbed the spot where the blade had dug into my flesh. "You could have fooled me," I mumbled.

"Again?" he asked.

When I looked up at Aerden's face, black smoke swirled around him like a tornado. I swallowed, narrowing my eyes at him.

"You sure you're all right?" I asked.

"I'm fine," he said through clenched teeth. Where his form usually looked clear and distinct when we were sparring, today he looked like he was cloaked in shadows. Dark smoke swirled all around him in fast, uneven circles. "Are we going again or not?"

He was definitely not fine.

"I can't," I said. "I don't want to be late for the rehearsal."

He kicked a rock at the edge of the water and it burst into flames so hot it melted and oozed over the side.

I'd never seen him act like this before, but the closer we'd gotten to the day of my engagement ceremony, the more his attitude had soured. Whenever I tried to talk to him about it, though, he refused to talk.

I bent down to collect my shirt and weapons and happened to look up just as Aerden lifted a large black rock. He reared back and threw it at me with even greater speed than he'd thrown the fireball.

I barely shifted in time to avoid a major concussion.

The rock passed through my shadow and I pushed through the air toward him, anger surging through my veins.

"What the hell was that for?" I asked, reforming and getting up in his face.

"What do you mean?" he asked, meeting my gaze with a look of steel.

"I mean, I told you I was done for the day. You've been in a crappy mood all morning," I said. "Do you want to talk about this? Or are you going to keep pretending you don't care?"

He turned his face away and walked over to where we'd left a few canisters of spring water.

"Fine," I said, turning my back on him. "Don't talk to me about it. I'm done."

He raised his canister above him and guzzled down half the water in a few seconds. He didn't even look over at me.

"Aerden, I'm serious about this," I said, not wanting to leave things like this between us. "I didn't ask to be chosen for this. I'll gladly hand it over to you if that's what you want."

He cut his eyes toward me, his lip curled up in a grimace. "That's not how it works and you know it."

I raised an eyebrow and crossed my arms in front of me. "So, I was right. You are upset about this," I said.

He turned away again, but this time, I grabbed his shoulder and spun him toward me.

Aerden pushed my hand off of his arm and stood, taking two angry steps toward me.

"Get off me," he said. His breath was heavy, his chest rising and falling rapidly with each inhale and exhale.

"Hey, don't put this on me," I said. "If you're jealous, you're going to have to either talk about it or learn to deal with it. You might have centuries before I take over as king, but you only have a few hours until it's too late for me to say no."

His head snapped toward me. "You think I'm upset about you becoming king someday?"

I stepped backward. "What else would you be so mad about?"

His face softened and he looked away from me, avoiding my eyes.

I shook my head, trying to make sense of his anger. What was really going on here?

I walked toward him and rested my hand on his arm. "Listen, I don't want to fight with you. You're my twin brother," I said. "You're the most important person in the world to me. I don't want this to come between us, but if you don't tell me what's eating you up, how can I understand?"

Aerden's mouth fell open and he sucked in a nervous breath.

But just when I thought he might finally open up to me, small arms wrapped around my waist and pulled me backward.

I closed my eyes and took a deep breath before turning to Lazalea.

"Hey Lea," I said.

She giggled and lifted her face to me, her green eyes bright and shining with happiness. "Hi," she said. "I thought I might find you two out here playing around."

I cleared my throat and pulled her arms away from me, but when I turned back to Aerden, I saw his eyes lingering on her soft hands.

And then I knew.

The realization of it took my breath away, leaving a heavy feeling in my chest.

I stared at him and when his eyes flicked up toward mine, I saw what I'd been missing all this time. All these years. How could I have been so blind?

Aerden wasn't upset I was going to be king.

He was upset I was going to marry the woman he loved.

TORN

"Come on," Lea said. She grabbed my hand and squeezed, but when I saw jealousy flash in my brother's eyes, I realized he saw every touch as a betrayal.

I released her hand as if it were on fire.

"Aerden and I were just finishing up a game. Can I meet you later?" I asked.

Lea's shoulders fell and worry wrinkled her forehead. "Is everything okay?"

I glanced toward my brother, who had turned his back on us.

"Everything's fine," I said. "There's just been a lot going on lately, and I wanted to spend some time with Aerden today since it might be our last chance to do this kind of thing for a while."

She shook her head. "Denaer, there's no time, your mother said she needs to see you right away," she said, then bit her lower lip and smiled. "She needs to give you something."

Aerden's head turned toward us and I swallowed hard.

"Hold on," I told her.

I walked over to my brother. "I need to talk to you," I said. "Can we meet up later?"

"I have a lot going on right now, too," he said with a shrug. "Let's just wait and see what happens."

I wished we had more time. Why didn't he tell me he loved her? If he'd said something years ago, or even months ago, maybe we could have done something about it. Maybe we could have switched places.

Lea's eyes met mine and she sucked in a breath. "Are you coming?"

A strange twinge tugged at my heart.

What choice did I have?

I took her hand, suddenly torn between duty and loyalty.

HEART STONES

WHEN I GOT home, my mother was waiting for me in my room.

"Where have you been?" she asked. She wore long red robes with ribbons of silver embedded in the fabric. On her head, she wore a crown of silver adorned with red and yellow stones. It was a mark of nobility, earned through my father's position on the king's council. "There's still so much that needs to get done before tomorrow."

"I was sparring with Aerden outside the city," I said.

"You know you don't have time for things like that anymore," she said with a frown. "You're going to have a lot of responsibilities coming up."

I sighed. "That's exactly why I wanted to spend some extra time with him," I said. "He hasn't been himself lately."

I didn't say anything about his feelings for Lea. I wanted to talk to him about it first.

Worry flashed in my mother's eyes for a moment, but it disappeared just as quickly. A smile spread across her face and her shoulders straightened. "You know your brother," she said.

"He's very strong. He'll be fine. Besides, Aerden should be the least of your concerns right now."

I sat down in a chair beside the window, suddenly feeling so tired.

"I'm glad you're here now," she said. She placed her hand on my shoulder. "There's something very important we need to talk about."

She reached inside her robes to retrieve a small golden case.

My stomach twisted and I cleared my throat. "What's that?"

Mother smiled and held the locket out to me. "Open it," she said.

I took it in my hand, expecting the metal to be cool to the touch. Instead, it was warm and smooth. I turned it over in my hands, searching for some kind of clasp, but it was smooth like a stone. "How?"

"Set it in the palm of your hand, then wave your other hand over the top of it like this." She showed me the motion.

I imitated her and the case opened slowly, like the petals of a growing flower. I studied the clear, colorless stone inside. I'd never seen anything like it before. In our world, we had stones of almost every color imaginable, but I'd never seen one with no color at all.

"Diamonds are one of the rarest stones," she said. "Rare, but pure and very powerful."

"What is it for?"

She sat down in the chair across from me and put her hand on mine.

"The exchanging of heart stones is one of the most honored and secret traditions in the engagement ceremony," she said. "The stone has been cleansed and blessed with a special spell. As soon as you hold it in your hand and think of your chosen mate, the stone will pull the truth of your feelings for her straight from your heart."

I stared down at the diamond. It was small, but I could feel the power radiating from it. The air around us buzzed with it.

"I don't understand," I said. "What's the purpose of it?"

"Promising yourself to another is more than an act of obedience," she said. "Even though this match was arranged for you, the engagement itself must be a choice you both make. The heart stones help you make that final decision to commit your lives to each other."

I shook my head, still not understanding.

My mother smiled. "The princess has been given a matching stone," she said. "You will each pour your true feelings for each other into the heart stones. Your love. Your doubt. Your adoration. Whatever the stone feels is most important. Then, during the ceremony, you and Princess Lazalea will exchange these stones under a veil of privacy. You will open them in front of each other, each seeing what the other placed inside. She will know your true heart and you, my son, will know hers."

The truth of what she was saying hit me like the crushing weight of a mountain on my chest. I couldn't speak or breathe.

If Lea saw my true feelings, she would know that I didn't love her.

"I can't do this," I said. I handed the golden locket back to my mother and stood up. I wanted to get as far away from that glimmering stone as I could.

My mother followed me toward the other side of the room. "You must," she said, handing it out to me. "It's part of the tradition."

I shook my head and pressed my palm against the cool black wall.

"Darling, there's nothing to be nervous about," she said, patting my back. "What secrets could you possibly have from one another? The two of you have been inseparable since you were shadowlings. She already knows how you feel about her."

I closed my eyes, my heart beating so fast it made my head spin. Yes, Lea and I had been inseparable, but she had no idea what my true feelings were. Of course, I cared for her as a friend, but I knew I didn't love her the way she wanted to be loved.

I had watched her affection for me growing over the years and I had truly done everything in my power to make myself feel the same way. We'd been promised to each other at birth and because of it, I resigned myself to a life without love a long time ago.

But I never wanted her to know that. I wanted her to feel loved. She deserved that.

Knowing what I knew now about Aerden's feelings only made this more complicated.

There had to be a way to make this right.

"Why?" I asked, turning to my mother. "Why are you just now giving me the stone? Why didn't someone tell me about this sooner?"

"Denaer, I don't understand why you're so upset about this." Her face twisted with worry. "The stone must be presented at the last minute like this so that there can be no chance to alter the stone's truth. It's tradition for the couple to pour their hearts into the stone on the day before the engagement. It remains secret so that it remains pure."

I forced myself to breathe, but my heart ached inside its cage.

"Does anyone ever open the locket and change their mind?" I asked. "What if someone found out the person they were matched with didn't love them? What then?"

She grabbed my hand from my side and pressed the golden locket into my palm. "What you see inside the heart stone can be your greatest joy or your darkest secret," she said, her gaze piercing through me. "But rejecting a match this important would bring shame to everyone."

I closed my fist around the case and nodded.

I understood her completely. Lea would never reject this match and shame her family. Instead, she would see the truth inside the heart stone. She would have to live the rest of her life knowing I didn't love her.

I would become her darkest secret.

I couldn't let that happen when I knew that there was someone else who truly loved her.

I needed to find Aerden.

ALREADY TOO LATE

I FOUND HIM BY the water at the edge of the Black Cliffs. Some days, the surface of the water looked like glass, black, and shining and so smooth it looked as if one could walk across it.

But today, the waves were wild and stormy. Any demon who went into the water today would be dragged under, never to be seen again. He would spend an eternity being tossed around at the bottom of the sea, every second a struggle.

I have known since I was a small child that I was meant to marry Princess Lazalea. Back then, I didn't care one way or another. I knew nothing of love or hope or freedom. All I knew was loyalty and obligation.

Marrying her was my duty, and I was ready to do as I was told.

But now, as the day of our engagement ceremony approached, I felt as restless as the sea.

Seeing my brother there beside the stormy shore, his face shrouded in dark hurt, I suddenly wondered if going through with the engagement would condemn us both to a life fighting the waves. A life of darkness and struggle under a sea of glass.

I made my way to him slowly, unsure what I should say.

The solution was complicated, because there was more than just my feelings or Aerden's to consider.

Lea was my friend, but where I didn't feel a passionate love for her, I knew she felt something much deeper for me. I could feel it in the soft touch of her hand against mine. It was there every time she looked into my eyes. She loved me. She wanted to spend eternity by my side.

Even if I didn't feel the same way for her, I thought I could make a life with her. I could be a good mate for her, never revealing to her that my feelings weren't as strong. But now?

Now she would know.

The truth would bring her pain I wasn't prepared to inflict.

Seeing the love and sorrow in my brother's eyes only made things worse for all of us.

If he loved her, how would he ever forgive me for marrying her? My engagement to Lea would create an impossible distance between us. Our relationship would never be the same, and I wasn't sure I could survive that. My brother was a part of me in a way no one else could understand.

I couldn't live the rest of my life knowing I'd brought so much pain to them both.

I approached Aerden with a heavy heart.

He tensed at my presence, not even bothering to turn around and meet my eyes. Instead, he continued to look out over the rough seas.

"Leave me alone," he said.

I sat down next to him on the edge of the cliff.

"Why didn't you tell me?" I asked.

He closed his eyes briefly, then sighed and ran a hand through his hair. "I don't know what you're talking about."

"Bullshit," I said. "This is it, Aerden. We're out of time. You either start being honest with me—with yourself—or you're going to regret this for the rest of your life."

He let his head fall into his hands and I placed my palm flat and sure against his shoulder.

"You have to tell her how you feel before it's too late," I said.

"It's already too late, can't you see that?" he said. "I'm not the one she loves."

I swallowed a thick lump in my throat. "If you don't speak now, then you'll have to live the rest of your days wondering what might have happened if you'd told her the truth."

"If I tell her the truth, I'll have to live all my days knowing that even though she knew how I felt, she still chose you," he said. He looked up, his blue eyes filled with tears.

"You don't know that," I said. "Maybe she only loves me because she feels she has to."

He pressed his lips together, anger evident in the sharp inhale.

"Everyone knows," he said. "It's obvious in the way she looks at you. The way she touches you."

I wanted to tell him it wasn't true, but how could I?

"I can't let this come between us," I said. "I won't."

Aerden snorted and straightened his shoulders. "What will you do, then, brother? Refuse to marry her?"

"Maybe," I said, lifting my chin. "I would do that if you asked me to."

"And shame our parents? Defy the King of the North?" He laughed. "You don't have the nerve. Besides, you'd break her heart."

His eyes darkened again and he went back to staring at the ocean.

"I'm going to break her heart, anyway," I said. I held the golden locket out for him to see.

"What's that?" he asked.

I explained the secret of the heart stones and his eyes filled with shadows.

"We have to tell her the truth before it's too late," I said. "If we both go to her and explain our feelings now, we can leave it for her to decide. It's the only way."

"No," he said, standing. "She would still choose you, can't you see that?"

"You don't know that." I stood and put my hand on his arm, but he pulled away from me.

"I do," he said, "and if you don't, then you're blind. I'd rather carry this secret inside me until the day of my passing then have to go through that. If you can't understand that, then you don't know me at all."

"I know you better than anyone in this world or the next," I said. "And what I saw in your eyes this morning when you looked at her nearly broke my own heart. Why can't you just put aside your pride and tell her how you feel?"

"You can't even begin to understand how difficult this has been for me," Aerden said, his voice echoing against the rocky cliffs. "Every single time I'm with her, I struggle not to tell her how I feel. I fight against my own heart, begging not to feel this way for someone who is promised to another. Then, when I see the way she looks at you..."

He walked three or four steps along the jagged edge of the cliff. The look of longing in his eyes when he stared down at the water sent a ripple of fear through my spine.

"I can't do this to you," I said. "I can't see this sorrow in your eyes for the rest of my days, knowing I was the cause of it."

"You won't have to," he said.

The slight tremble in his voice unnerved me. "What do you mean?"

He clenched his teeth and his jaw rippled with tension. "Nothing," he said.

My stomach twisted tight. "Tell me," I said.

"I've been thinking about going away for a while," he said.

I shook my head, not wanting to believe this could be true. "Where?" I asked. "For how long?"

Aerden picked up a stone and tossed it into the raging waves below. "As long as it takes," he said. "Maybe forever."

The world fell out from under my feet. "Aerden—"

"Don't try to talk me out of it," he said. "I've been thinking about this for a long time. It's what I need to do. Maybe if I spent some time traveling, I would find something more to live for. Maybe I could forget about her."

"There has to be another way," I said. "I'll tell her the truth. I'll tell her I don't love her, but that you do. I'll tell her I can't marry her, but that you'll marry her in my place. In time, she will learn to love you."

"No," Aerden said. "It's not your place to tell her how I feel."

"This can't be the way our lives go," I said. "You're a part of me. You're my other half."

He hardened his expression. "No," he said. "We are separate. We're not children anymore and the time has come for us to stand up and accept the choices that have been made for us. They chose you, Denaer, and there's nothing we can do to change that."

"Where will you go?" I asked. "How will I reach you?"

"I met a woman who said she knows of a place where my magic will be appreciated," he said. "It sounded amazing. I think it's what I need right now."

"What woman?" I asked, panic flowing through me. "Where did you meet her?"

He sighed. "Let's talk about this another time," he said. "I'd really like to be alone for a while."

"Promise me you won't go anywhere before I've had a chance to say goodbye," I said. "Promise me you'll be there tomorrow for the ceremony."

Aerden placed his hand firmly against my arm. "I'll be there. I promise," he said. "But I want you to promise me something, too."

"Anything," I said.

"Promise me you will try to love her," he said, his eyes filling with tears. "She deserves that."

"I will," I said.

He pulled me into a hug, then turned away.

I left him there at the edge of the Black Cliffs, a dark feeling swirling in my stomach.

SHE WILL NEVER HAVE TO KNOW

I TOSSED AND TURNED throughout the night.
When I finally fell asleep, I dreamed of the sea. And when I woke, I felt restless.

I knew I didn't have much time until the preparations for today's ceremonies would begin, and I still hadn't put my feelings into the heart stone.

I had left the golden locket on the table beside the window, but when I went to retrieve it, it was gone.

I searched every corner of my room, and when I realized it was nowhere to be found, I collapsed onto my bed.

Where could I have left it?

I'd been so sure it was there by the window.

Then, a thought tugged at my brain and I stood.

Aerden.

I shifted and flew through my rooms as fast as I could, traveling through the long corridor that connected our two towers.

His room was a twin of my own, situated up a long staircase and at the top of a tower. We each had a suite of rooms including a bedroom, bathroom, closet, and small welcoming room.

He usually kept his outer door closed, but as I reached the top of the stairs, his door stood wide open. An uneasy feeling knotted in my stomach.

With heavy steps, I entered his room, praying this was all in my head. I told myself I'd see him sitting at his breakfast table, fully dressed and ready to face the day.

But I already knew he was gone.

I could feel his absence.

We'd always had an incredibly strong bond. Even when we weren't together, I was always connected to him, as if he were simply an extension of me.

Sometimes when we sparred, I could sense his movements before he made them. I could anticipate his thoughts.

But when I focused in on his energy now, I couldn't sense him anywhere.

A cold vine wrapped around my spine, and I shivered. I walked through the entryway and into his bedroom.

There, on the table near his bed, was the golden locket. Underneath, he'd left a note. My eyes filled with tears as I sat down, the note clutched in my trembling hand.

Dear brother,

I have broken my promise to you, and I hope that you will find it in your heart to forgive me.

I cannot stay in this city and watch the kingdom celebrate your happiness while my own heart is breaking. I'm not sure I could survive the pain.

But I also couldn't live with the pain of knowing Lea's heart had also been broken.

You said telling her the truth was the only way to make things right, but I found another way. A better way that will give her great joy and allow you to both be happy together.

When she opens the heart stone inside this locket, Lea will see that she is loved. She will understand how much she means in this world, and it won't matter that it was my love instead of yours. She will never have to know.

All she needs to know is that the love inside the stone is pure and true.

Please let me do this for her. For both of you.

I don't know how long I'll be gone or where I'm going, but I will reach out to you when I can. Someday, if my heart can heal, I will come home and stand by your side.

I love you, brother.
 -Aerden.

I DIDN'T DESERVE HER

OCTOBER 31, 2013

A KNOCK ON THE door startled me out of my memories of the distant past, bringing me back to my bedroom at Brighton Manor. I let the memory stone fall back into my pocket and took a deep breath as the images of that day so long ago faded away.

The door cracked open slightly and Harper stuck her head just inside the door. The smile on her face radiated warmth and happiness, dispersing some of the cold anger and regret in my heart.

"Hey, sexy," she said. "Can I come in?"

My hand absently brushed the stone in my pocket and I nodded. "Of course."

She opened the door and slipped inside, then shut it behind her.

The sight of her took my breath away. Her blond hair had grown longer over the past few months, but tonight she was wearing it up in beautiful, thick braids that coiled around her head. A beautiful white rose was placed near her temple and she wore band of beads around her forehead like a crown.

We'd decided not to completely abandon Peachville's tradition of an annual Halloween Ball. This year, though, no one from the Order of Shadows was invited.

Harper and I had decided to go as a couple from a silent film we'd watched together. My costume was easy. All I'd needed was a tuxedo.

But Harper had gone all out. Her dress was a shiny satin that hugged all of her curves. She wore several long layers of pearls that draped perfectly across her body and swayed as she walked toward me. Nestled between the pearls, she still wore her mother's locket, too, even though the magic inside it had been extinguished along with all of the blue portals.

"You look incredible," I said, reaching for her and pulling her into my arms.

"And you look half-dressed," she said with a laugh as she snuggled against my cheek. "What have you been doing up here all this time?"

I shrugged and look down at the discarded bow tie on my dresser. "I couldn't figure out how to tie this stupid thing," I said. I felt slightly guilty lying to her, but I couldn't tell her the real thoughts that had occupied my mind for the past half hour. I wanted to have all of the memories inside the stone before I told her about it.

"Here, let me," she said.

She picked up the tie and moved her arms around my neck, lifting my collar and placing the bow tie in the right position.

"Since when did you learn how to tie a bow tie?" I asked.

She smiled and the sight of her cherry red lips made my neck flush with warmth.

"I didn't," she said.

Then, she stepped back and closed her eyes. With a simple wave of her hand, my tie moved on its own, twisting around until it was tied into the perfect bow.

I smiled and studied it in the mirror.

"A glamour?" I asked.

"Not exactly," she said. "Just something I've been working on."

I shook my head and wrapped my arms around her waist. Her dress dipped low in the back and I placed my palm flat against her bare skin, so grateful for the warmth of her body against mine.

I lowered my lips toward hers, but at the last moment, she placed a finger against my lips and shook her head.

"This lipstick is real, I'll have you know," she said. "No glamour tonight. If you kiss me now, you're going to look like a clown instead of a handsome movie star."

"It's worth it," I said, dipping to kiss her again.

She giggled and squirmed out of my arms.

I laughed and watched her practically float away. She placed her hand on the heavy wooden door and turned back toward me before she left.

"Don't be long," she said. "Almost everyone's here already."

I blew her a kiss and she pretended to catch it before she disappeared into the hallway.

I touched my hand to the stone in my pocket, thinking how I never dreamed I would ever love someone as much as I love her.

And how I was certain I didn't deserve her.

THE BEGINNING OF THE TERROR

I WANTED NOTHING MORE than to join her and our friends downstairs, but there was still work to be done. I reached in my pocket and took out the stone again.

All my memories of the days leading up to the engagement ceremony were just the very beginning of the story.

When I found Aerden's note and the golden case that held the heart stone, I mourned his absence, but at the same time, a part of me understood why he did what he did. He was willing to sacrifice his own happiness so that Lea and I could find happiness, but he didn't want to stay behind and watch us together every single day.

I understood why he had to go.

But knowing he was gone was only the beginning of the terror that was to come.

I closed my hand around the stone and let my memories drift back to that day just over a hundred years ago.

IT CANNOT BE UNDONE
THE SHADOW WORLD, 101 YEARS AGO

I CRUMBLED AERDEN'S NOTE between my fingers, then slammed my fist against the table.

How could I have let this happen? Yesterday, I felt that something was wrong. I knew he was acting distant. I should have kept an eye on him. I should have demanded he talk to Lea himself.

I let my head fall against the table.

I felt empty and alone. How could I live without him?

In the light, something shimmered and caught my eye near his bed. I walked over, dread pooling in my core. I pulled up a blanket that had slid onto the floor on the opposite side of the bed.

Aerden's axe lay discarded on the stone floor.

He would never have left this here. He went everywhere with that axe. Aerden was a warrior by nature, always ready for any situation or danger. He wouldn't have gone on some grand adventure without it.

I picked it up and as soon as my hand touched the silver, a vision flashed before my eyes.

It came to me in pieces, as these kinds of visions often did.

Seeing the future was one of my gifts, handed down from generations before me. The older I got, the stronger my visions had become, but they were rarely full scenes. Mostly, they were more like images in my head. Fragments of a greater whole.

In this vision, Aerden stood in a circle of black roses, a glowing mass of light hovering just above the ground.

My hands curled into tight fists around the axe's handle, and I strained to see more before the vision faded. But the harder I tried to hold onto it, the faster it slipped away.

When it had disappeared completely from my mind's eye, I stood, my brother's axe clutched tight in my hand. Terror began to grow within me. I had to find him. I needed to warn him.

I closed my eyes and tried to feel my connection with him like we'd done a thousand times. When I was scared or lonely, I could always reach out to him. His presence was always with me, even if we were miles apart.

Our connection wasn't something you could see. It was more of a feeling. A knowing. Something that couldn't be described in words, but something that we'd always had.

At that moment, I sent a piece of my spirit out to him, wanting to know that wherever he had gone, he was still with me.

But for the first time in our fifty years of life, I couldn't reach him.

There was no reassuring presence. No connection. There was only distance.

I grabbed the axe and the locket, then flew out of his room and down the stairs. I had no idea where to look, but I had to try. The engagement could be postponed. Lea would understand.

There was no way to know how long Aerden had before this came to pass. Sometimes my visions came to pass within days. Others had still never come true even after years of waiting.

Even if this was a vision of the distant future, I knew I needed to find him and tell him what I'd seen. Maybe there was still a chance I could make things right. A chance I could save him from this fate.

When I burst through the door of my room, though, I found my mother waiting in the entryway.

"Denaer?" She looked from my eyes to the axe and back again. "What's going on?"

I hesitated. My gift of visions had been one her father had passed down. She'd asked me to never share these visions with her. She'd said there was no way to change them once you'd seen them, so she saw no point in letting them rule your actions.

Still, this was important.

"It's Aerden," I said. "He's gone."

I walked past her into the bedroom. A light breeze blew in through the open archway and on the streets below, I could already hear the sounds of the crowd gathering for today's celebration.

"What do you mean, he's gone?" she asked, following me.

I pulled a large leather bag from my closet and began filling it with weapons and clothing.

"What are you doing?" She placed herself between me and the bag, then put her hand on my arm. "Stop. You've gone mad."

I didn't have time for this. I threw the clothes on the floor, then reached into my pocket and took out the golden case. "When I woke up this morning, the locket was gone," I said.

She shook her head, confusion wrinkling her forehead. "Where was it?"

"In Aerden's room," I said.

"You're not making any sense," she said. "Why would your heart stone be in Aerden's room?"

"Because he's the one who is in love with the princess," I said. I knew it wasn't my secret to tell, but I needed to make her understand what was going on. "I have never loved Lea. Not the way he does."

My mother fell back against the bed. "You don't mean that," she said.

"Yes, I do," I said. "I was willing to marry her because it was my duty, but yesterday I realized how blind I'd been to Aerden's feelings for her. I tried to tell him to go to her and tell her how he feels, but he refused. Instead, he filled the heart stone in my place and left."

"Where did he go?" she asked.

"I don't know," I said. "But I have to find him."

"Wait," she said, gripping my arm so tight, it burned. "You can't go anywhere. Not today. There's no time. We have to be at the castle soon."

I shook my head and continued packing. "I had a vision," I said. "I know you don't want to hear about them, but this time, what I saw makes me think Aerden's in trouble. I have to warn him."

She lowered her head into her hands for a long moment while I rushed around the room, gathering supplies.

Finally, she raised her chin. "It doesn't matter what you saw," she said. "Once a vision has been seen, it cannot be undone. There's nothing you can do for him now."

I didn't want to listen to her. What if there was a way? "I have to try."

She grabbed my arm and pushed me toward the window. "Look down there," she said. "There are thousands of demons who have traveled great distances to be here for this ceremony today. If you leave now, you will shame us all."

I stared out of the window, my stomach twisting with regret. I should have never let things get this far.

From the looks of it, the entire kingdom had come to witness the ceremony.

The King of the North had been known as one of the greatest kings of all time and the demons of the Northern Kingdom loved him with a ferocious passion. When Lazalea was born nearly fifty years ago, the people had come from all over the kingdom to send prayers of love and light into the sky in celebration.

She was their great hope for the future and they loved her just as much as they had always loved her father.

I could see it in the eyes of the demons in the street below. They all shared looks of joy and love, their loyalty to the royal family so true and resolved.

Seeing the villagers who had traveled so far to be here to witness our promise ceremony, it suddenly hit me how significant this moment really was.

How much it would hurt everyone if I walked away.

I leaned against the wall, feeling so defeated and lost.

"In time, your brother will learn to live with his sorrow, and when he does, he will come back to us. Just wait and see. He has made a great sacrifice for you today," she said. "For both of you. Honor him by doing what is right and following through with your commitments. Bringing shame on all of us will not do him any good. Either way, he was going to lose her. You have to see that."

I lifted my head and looked at my mother. She was a good woman, but at that moment, for the first time in my life, I understood that she cared more for her place in this kingdom than she did for the happiness of her own children.

I would find no sympathy in her eyes.

"Come, Mother."

I stood and held my arm out to her, resolved to my fate even as my heart was breaking.

She nodded and wrapped her arms around me.

"Thank you," she said, whispering against my forehead as she hugged me close.

WHAT WAS EXPECTED OF ME

THE WALK TO the castle was like a funeral march. Every step had weight, as if my shoes were filled with sand and stone. I wanted to reach back in time and take it back, but it was too late.

I had to find a way to be strong.

I thought of my brother sitting alone in his room in the early morning hours, pouring his love into the heart stone, knowing that the woman he loved would believe they were my feelings.

What kind of strength did that take? What did it feel like to love someone so much you would sacrifice everything to make them happy and keep them from pain?

I would never know that same kind of love.

My parents had taken that chance away from me the moment I was born into this world.

My mother's hand squeezed my arm and when I turned to meet her gaze, her eyes widened, reminding me I had a role to play.

We paused just outside the archway that led into the throne room. We had been through these steps a dozen times in the past month, and I knew exactly what was expected of me.

I buried my regrets and my worry deep inside, then straightened my shoulders.

There was no use going through it all in my head over and over. This was my destiny, and I would embrace it with courage and strength.

As I looked on the faces of the demons sitting in the throne room, I vowed to put aside my own selfish desires. I would dedicate my life to the kingdome. I would do whatever it took to honor my brother by becoming the mate Lea deserved.

Somewhere high above, bells rang to signal the beginning of the ceremony.

An excited hush fell over the gathered crowd.

My mother's grip on my arm tightened and I swallowed down my regrets and my secrets.

The doors to the king's chamber room opened on the opposite side of the hall, and all eyes focused on the light streaming through from the royal chambers.

A chorus of shadowlings poured forth from somewhere in the back of the room, their ethereal forms swirling and dancing upon the air. They flew around both sides of the throne, floating high up toward the ceiling.

A single shadowling girl took form on the bottom step leading up toward the platform. Her voice flowed from her, a sound so heart-breakingly pure no one dared breathe or move as they listened.

She sang in an ancient demon language, long abandoned in our daily lives, but still used on occasions of great importance.

Even though I'd studied the language in my lessons when I was younger, I could only understand a few words of her song, its meaning was clear. It was a song about the beauty of love.

When she was through the first verse, the rest of the shadowlings joined her on the stairs, adding their voices to the song. Music filled the chamber, echoing from every corner, a harmony so pure and perfect it brought tears to my eyes.

From the back of the room, a parade of priestesses made their way down the center of the crowd, colorful flames dancing in the air above their cupped hands.

Behind them, the king's council passed through the crowd. They wore robes of gold and deep red. My father held a position of honor at the front of the procession. When he came into view, my mother straightened and smiled, pride radiating from her.

Did it not matter to her at all that her other son was completely missing from the ceremony? When had her ambitions grown so high?

Or had my parents always valued their position in the court this highly?

I had been so blind. I was a child until today and suddenly, I wished I never had to grow up. I would rather have spent the rest of my life playing in the fields with my brother and Lea than have had my eyes ripped open to these harsh truths.

My father's eyes sought mine across the heads of the demons seated in the front rows. He lowered his head in a brief nod and I nodded back, accepting my role.

The priestesses bowed to the empty throne, then split off into two groups, one going left and the other right. They turned around to face the crowd, then in perfect unison, lifted their arms. Their flames lifted high into the air above our heads, then moved together to form a circle just above the throne. The flames spun faster as they moved closer together, finally coming together to form a single bright flame. Its light shone down across the golden floor before the throne.

I drew in a breath, knowing this was where I was meant to stand and pledge my heart and my life to Lea.

The song of the shadowlings ended and the throne room fell into a reverent silence.

A row of musicians in the balcony at the back of the hall lifted glass horns to their lips and began the royal processional.

The crowd of demons knelt and bowed their head as the king and queen appeared from their chambers.

The king stepped to the edge of the steps and raised his hands high into the air. At his command, everyone stood. He smiled and lowered his head in acknowledgment and praise. Excitement rippled through the air.

The King of the North led his queen back toward the throne. He kissed her hand, then left her side as they took their positions on either side of the golden throne. They turned their gaze toward the door to their chambers and my breath hitched in my throat. I struggled to stand tall and confident when all I wanted to do was turn and run like a scared little kid.

My eyes were glued to the light in the archway.

When Princess Lazalea appeared, my eyes widened. From where I stood, I saw her before the rest of the crowd, and I understood their gasps as she made her way to the light in front of her parents.

She looked like a being from another world. Her gown was a deep red velvet adorned with golden rings that shimmered when she walked. On her head, she wore a golden circlet with a single red jewel that hung down between her eyes like a teardrop.

When she was in place, she lowered her head, then slowly lifted her eyes toward the archway where I stood.

Her eyes met mine and a smile played at the corners of her mouth.

For a moment, I couldn't react or respond. The joy and adoration in her expression was one of a lover. I'd never seen her look at me that boldly before, and I didn't know if it was new or if my eyes were finally seeing what had always been there.

That was when I fully understood why Aerden wouldn't let me tell her the truth.

The truth would have destroyed her.

The trumpets stopped and an orchestra of strings began to play. I recognized the music from rehearsals, and I had to force my feet forward.

As I passed the council members, I kept my eyes forward, only stopping briefly to bow to my father out of respect. My father lowered his head toward me, then set his hand on my shoulder. The weight of it was heavy, reminding me of my duty to my family and my kingdom.

Aerden should have been sitting in the front row, but I didn't allow myself to look at his empty seat.

I had to be strong now for both of us.

When I got to the center of the room, I stopped at the bottom of the steps and knelt down before the king and queen. As I bowed my head, I thought of Aerden. I tried again to reach him through our connection.

This time, instead of the vast emptiness I'd felt earlier, I was overcome by a violent fear. But as soon as it had come, it was gone again.

I nearly stumbled as I tried to stand. A few in the crowd gasped and I felt my father's eyes bearing down on me. I lifted my eyes to Lea and her smile faltered. She shook her head in confusion, but I couldn't tell her what I'd experienced. All I could do was push back my fear and ascend the steps toward her.

Her chest rose and fell with long breaths as she placed her smile back on her face.

My eyes flickered to her hands. She had her fist clasped around something small, and I knew she was holding onto her locket with the heart stone inside.

What would I see when I opened it?

All I could think about was how much I wished it were Aerden standing here instead of me. I wished he had been chosen instead of me.

When I took my place at Lea's side, all I wanted in the whole world was to rewind to a time when it was just the three of us playing in the fields as friends. I yearned for a life with no expectations or responsibilities.

But as her hand reached for mine, I knew that we couldn't stop time. We would never be able to hold onto the days of the past. Life kept moving forward, for better or worse and the best any of us could do was try to find a way to be happy with the life fate had handed us.

THE VEIL

THE CEREMONY CONTINUED in a blur. Some part of me must have heard the words, because I felt my body going through all the right motions. I answered at all the right times. I smiled when Lea smiled, reassuring her even as I myself needed reassurances.

I felt the eyes of every demon in the room on the two of us, their hopes and dreams of a prosperous future affixed on our joined hands.

I was both there and not there.

And when it came time for us to exchange truth stones, I handed her mine with the confidence of a demon in love. My hands did not tremble. My eyes never wavered from hers for a second.

But inside a hidden part of myself, I guarded a dark secret. The most terrible lie a man can tell a woman.

A part of me changed that day. Even before I knew the truth about what had happened to Aerden, I knew the course of our lives had gone severely off track. One wrong decision led to another and another until I found myself standing in front of a princess, promising her something that was never mine to give.

She took the golden locket from my hand, her eyes shining with hope.

Lea, the confident girl I'd grown up with, someone who never showed a single weakness or moment of doubt, shivered with fear as the priestess summoned the veil that would hide us from the hopeful eyes of the crowd around us.

A shimmering light surrounded us, flowing up like a curtain of stars.

We stood facing each other in the light. Our lockets were clasped tight in our hands, but our eyes were locked together in anticipation.

In the days leading up to this moment, Lea and I had rarely spent any time alone. There had always been maidservants and family around us, preparing us for the ceremony. We hadn't had a chance to talk about what things might be like after we'd pledged our lives to one another.

But in the tradition of our elders, we were given this cocoon of light in which to confess our doubts and dreams. It was known as the last chance to reveal our true feelings and intentions. We could speak to each other without anyone outside hearing us or ever knowing what we'd shared.

This was the moment I could have told her the truth about my brother's feelings for her. I should have told her.

Only, seeing that tiny crack in her armor rattled me to the core.

Lea may act tough and strong, but for the first time, I saw that she was a woman, too.

"You go first," she said, her voice a whisper.

I cleared my throat and uncurled my fingers, laying the locket out flat against my palm. I took my eyes from hers and waved my free hand over the golden case.

I held my breath as it opened, revealing the small stone inside.

The light that spilled from it was strong and true. It wasn't blinding or brilliant, but it was honest.

I looked up into Lea's eyes and she smiled. Carefully, I lifted the stone from its velvet case and placed it near my heart as my mother had instructed. My eyes closed as her truth poured into me.

Through the magic of the stone, I saw myself through her eyes for the first time. She saw me as a dear friend, but there was so much more there than what I expected to see. She thought I was strong and compassionate. A warrior capable of winning battles, but also an artist able to see the beauty in small things.

She knew my love for my brother and in it, saw my loyalty to family. Because of this, she knew that I would be a good father someday.

Tears welled up in my eyes at these images that flowed through my mind and my heart.

I didn't deserve all this. I wasn't the honorable one she believed me to be.

When the stone was done showing me what was in her heart, I placed it back inside the golden case, closing it up again.

She looked at me with anticipation.

I didn't know what I was supposed to say.

"Thank you."

A puzzled look crossed her face. "Is that all you need to say?" she asked.

"Should there be more?"

She smiled and shook her head. "I don't know," she said. Then, she looked at the locket in her hand. "Can I open mine?"

I nodded.

Lea took a deep breath, then passed a hand over the locket, her fingers trembling.

I think I knew what to expect when it opened, but actually seeing it with my own eyes took my breath away.

A brilliant light poured from the small stone, so bright it made the stars inside the veil look dim.

Lea gasped, her breath hitching in her chest. She brought her free hand up to her mouth and tears spilled from her eyes. She took her time, watching the light sparkle in the space between us before she lifted it toward her heart.

Her eyes closed as the stone told her its secrets.

An ache gripped my chest as I watched her.

It should be Aerden standing here with her. Not me.

I would never know exactly what she saw inside that stone, but whatever it was touched her so deeply she nearly fell to her knees. I reached out for her, my arms slipping around her waist to hold her up.

She opened her eyes and in them, I saw so much love, it broke my heart into a million pieces.

"I didn't know," she said, searching my face. "Why didn't you tell me?"

I didn't have an answer for her.

She regained her footing and stepped back so she could put her stone away. She held the locket against her chest, her eyes flowing with tears. I'd never seen her cry before and it made me wish I loved her. I wanted to be able to give her true happiness instead of this lie.

"All this time, I was so afraid of opening the locket only to find that you were standing here out of obligation to your family and your king," she said with a laugh. She wiped her tears from her face. "I expected it, honestly. I prepared myself for it. But this? I never in a hundred years expected this. Is this how you have felt about me all this time?"

"Would you have accepted me anyway?" I asked, not wanting to answer her question. "Even if the stone hadn't been as bright?"

She smiled and threw her arms around me. "Yes," she whispered. "I have wanted you for as long as I have lived. Even the dimmest light from you would have meant more to me than the brightest stone from someone else."

I leaned my head against her shoulder. Her words cut deep into a part of me I hoped she would never have to see.

Aerden had been right, then.

Even if I'd told her the truth about his feelings, she would have chosen me instead.

But being right didn't justify the lie. The stone was a betrayal of the worst kind. I knew it the second its light reflected in her eyes.

I knew that someday, our desire to protect Lea from the truth would cause her more pain than truth ever could have.

A BLACK HOLE IN MY HEART

*I*N THE TRADITION of our people, the veil can only come down once the couple inside makes their decision about whether to part or to promise their future to each other.

If, after viewing the heart stones, either one of the couple decides to look for another partner, they are supposed to lay their locket on the floor at the other's feet, then turn their back. At this, the veil will fall into ash and they will both be released from their promise.

If they both choose to move forward with their engagement, the couple inside the veil must seal their promise with a kiss.

It's the final step in the engagement ceremony and the one I'd been dreading the most since my mother explained it to me.

Not that Lea wasn't a worthy mate. She was perfect and any demon in the kingdom would have been glad to trade places with me.

But in my mind, kissing her was like kissing a sister.

After the love she'd seen inside the stone, she'd be expecting something magical and passionate. A kiss to end all kisses. How could I possibly fake something like that?

I knew that our first kiss would be a lie and that every single kiss from here until eternity would be a betrayal. I would be lying to her, but also to myself. The weight of the future stretched out before me, but I knew we couldn't hide inside the veil forever.

Outside our cocoon, everyone was waiting.

I swallowed, my mouth suddenly dry.

"Lea..." I started, but couldn't finish.

She reached for my hands and I clung to her.

"Yes?" she asked.

I shook my head, feeling that I couldn't let this moment pass without trying one last time to reach out to my brother. I wanted him to know that even though we'd already exchanged stones, there was still time to tell her the truth if that's what he wanted from me. It wasn't too late.

I closed my eyes and lowered my head. When I exhaled, I sent a piece of myself out toward him, searching for that connection I'd never lived a day without.

I wasn't expecting to find him. Part of me knew he was long gone—disappeared to some place that had taken him farther than our bond could reach so that he wouldn't have to feel the pain of this day.

But there, at the very edge of my reach, I found him.

I was struck by the same terror I'd felt on the steps before. But this time, it didn't fade.

I felt his agony, but it was distant. At first, I was sure it was his loss of Lea that I was feeling. But when I reached further, my gut twisted and I was struck with a vision so powerful, it knocked me off my feet.

I fell to my knees and cried out as I felt the shackles around his wrists. The inside of them was filled with spikes that cut deep into his flesh. The pain was keeping him from shifting into his shadow form.

"What's wrong?" Lea's voice was panicked.

I was still holding tight to her hands and she knelt by my side, pulled down by the weight of my body.

Another vision struck me. Thorns pierced my brother's knees as he knelt on the ground. His clothing was ripped and bloodied. I pushed to the very limit of my ability, focused on nothing but the bond we shared as twins, determined not to let go of him. I had to let him know that I was here. That I was with him.

I heard Lea shouting, but I couldn't answer her.

My awareness had left the veil and I was transported to another place. A place I didn't recognize.

A field of black roses, arranged in a large circle around a dark blue orb of light.

In my vision, Aerden's head snapped up, almost as if he could see me.

He whispered my name as the sky above him grew dark as night. Someone stepped in front of the strange blue light. I struggled to see his face, but a badge across his arm flashed clear in my mind. A red dragon.

My strength began to fade, but I held on with everything I was.

And then, in a horrible instant, Aerden was ripped from me. It felt as if a blade had cut us apart, the pain of it so deep and so brutal, it slammed me against the ground. I screamed in terror as the vision disappeared.

Only, I suddenly knew with certainty that this wasn't a vision of the future.

I felt his absence from this world like a black hole in my heart, its darkness filling me with a loss so great I knew I would never recover.

I opened my eyes as Lea cradled my head against her lap, her hands stroking my face as she begged me to tell her what was happening.

"Aerden," I said, my voice hoarse from screaming. "Aerden's dead."

MORE THAN ENOUGH
THE HUMAN WORLD, PRESENT DAY

THE MEMORIES OF that horrible day tore through my mind like shards of glass.

I forced myself back to the present, releasing my grip on the memory stone. I didn't want to lose sight of all the good that had happened in my life since that day, but I also understood that none of this joy would have found me if it hadn't been for the pain of my past.

I focused on the sounds of the party beneath my room until my breathing calmed and the memories began to fade back into the past where they belonged.

There was so much more of the story to tell, but I needed to see my brother with my own eyes. I needed to know that he was here and he was safe. I stood and grabbed my jacket from the back of the chair, then opened the door and headed down the stairs to join the party.

I stood in the doorway of the living room for a long moment, silently watching my friends.

These were the people I held most dear to me in this world and the next.

Harper stood in the corner with a glass of red punch in her hand, whispering something to Mary Anne and Essex.

Mordecai, Joost, and Erick sorted through a collection of Cd's by the stereo.

Courtney sat in a chair that had been pushed against the wall, a book of spells open in her lap.

Lea was dressed in a white outfit with her hair pulled into two large buns. I brought my hand to my mouth, hiding my laughter as I realized she was dressed as Princess Leia from Star Wars. She danced in the center of the room with our friend Cristo.

And Aerden, the brother I thought had been stolen from me forever, stood against the far wall. In his human form, he looked almost identical to me except for the color of his eyes.

He must have sensed my presence, because the second my eyes landed on him, he looked up and smiled.

He shifted into a wisp of black smoke and in an instant, reappeared by my side. "What took you so long?" he asked. "I was beginning to wonder if you'd abandoned us."

"Never," I said, my tone more serious than I intended.

He studied me, then leaned against the door frame. "You're up to something."

I tried to keep from smiling but couldn't. "Maybe," I said.

"Definitely," he said. "And by the looks of it, whatever it is has put you in a less than partying mood."

I sunk my hand deep into my left pocket and twirled the golden case and the memory stone between my fingertips. "Can I ask you something?"

"Sure," he said.

"Have you given any thought to telling Lea the truth about the heart stone?"

He lowered his head, his hands falling to his sides. "I think it's too late for that, don't you?"

I shook my head. "I think it's never too late to tell someone the truth, no matter how scared you are."

He turned to watch her dancing. Even after a hundred years, his eyes still shone with his love for her. I really don't know how I didn't see it all those years ago.

"Lea and I don't belong together," he said. "We didn't a hundred years ago, and we still don't. Telling her about the stone would only open up old wounds."

"Maybe reopening those wounds is the only way to ever really heal them," I said.

Aerden swallowed and lowered his eyes again. "Lately I'm beginning to think her pain is the only thing holding her to this life," he said.

I drew in a deep breath. He was still trying to protect her.

Or maybe he was trying to protect himself.

Before I could ask him more, a hand slid around my waist. A slow smile crept across my face as Harper lay her head against my chest.

"When did you sneak down here?" she asked.

"Only a minute ago," I said. "Having fun?"

She looked around at our friends. "I think this is the first party I've been to where no one was murdered or kidnapped or dying. I call that a win, don't you?"

I laughed and wrapped my arms around her. "Yes, I do," I said.

"The night is still young," Aerden said, an eyebrow raised.

Harper rolled her eyes and leaned over to punch him in the arm. "Don't you jinx this, mister."

"Who? Me?" Aerden lifted his palms in the air and laughed. "If I remember correctly, I'm the one who saved you on more than one occasion such as this."

"Don't remind me," Harper said. Her hand absently gripped her blue pendant. It was nothing more than a pretty blue stone now, but she said it served as a reminder of how far she'd come and how much work was still to be done.

I think she just wore it to feel close to her mother.

"Well, I'll leave you two love birds alone," Aerden said. He pushed off the door frame and walked into the main hallway.

"Wait, where are you going?" I asked. There were still some things I needed to talk to him about before the night was over.

He shrugged and glanced toward the dance floor, sadness flashing in his eyes. "I need some air," he said, then took off toward the back door, leaving a trail of black smoke behind him.

"Do you think he's okay?" Harper asked, watching after him.

"I don't know," I said. "Every time I try to talk to him about the past, he brushes it off and then manages to avoid me for days. I wish he'd open up to me and tell me what he's thinking."

"Give him time," she said, taking my hand in hers and kissing the tip of my finger. "I can't imagine what it would have been like to be trapped inside someone else's soul for a hundred years. He's been through so much, Jackson. You can't expect him to get over all that in a matter of a few months."

I leaned down and kissed her forehead. "You really are amazing, you know that?"

She blushed and turned her head to the side. "So you keep telling me," she said. "I'll believe it when we've defeated the Order of Shadows for good."

I pulled away enough so I could see her eyes and know that she was truly listening to me. "Tonight isn't about them, okay?"

She was always so hard on herself. She'd managed to put the weight of two worlds on her shoulders as if she was personally responsible for saving every human and demon who had been hurt by the Order.

"It's Halloween. One hundred and one years since the Peachville gate was first opened," she said. "How can it not be about them?"

I smiled and and brushed the back of my hand along her soft cheek. "Because for the first time in over a hundred years, my brother is free and the gate is closed forever," I said. "You did that, Harper."

She leaned into my hand, closing her eyes as a tear escaped and ran a jagged path down her face. "It's not enough," she whispered.

"Look at me," I said.

Her eyelids fluttered open, revealing brown eyes shining with tears.

My heart overflowed with love and I pulled her tight against my chest. I remembered back to the hopelessness of the day Aerden disappeared. I remembered the party a year ago when Mrs. Ashworth had tried to take Harper's life. How the Order had followed us and taken Harper from me.

I thought the only two people I'd ever really loved had been lost to me forever.

"Yes it is," I said, my cheek pressed against her hair. "For tonight, it's more than enough."

A HIGH COST

LATER, I WENT searching for Aerden.
He'd been traveling in his shadow form, so I was able to follow him from the back door and into the woods by the line of decay he'd left in his wake.

In this world, using demon magic sucked the life from whatever it could use nearby. Plants, trees, animals, even humans. Something as simple as shifting didn't take much power, but my eye was trained to recognize even the slightest trail of demon magic.

I followed him out past the house I'd once shared with Ella Mae, across the field and into the woods, but the trail disappeared as I neared the ruins of the old Peachville demon gate.

Thinking I might find him near the destroyed portal, I walked the rest of the way to the clearing.

The ground beneath my feet still buzzed with the battle that had taken place here a few months ago. There had been so much death that day on all sides. Witches from the Peachville coven. Demons from the Resistance. Even Harper's father, the King of the South, had given his life in battle.

Our victory against Priestess Winter had come at a high cost, but the reward was immeasurable.

In the months following the battle, those of us who remained had started a new army—The Demon Liberation Movement. Our plan was to find the four remaining priestesses of the Order of Shadows and defeat them, one by one.

At first, we'd been high on hope, believing we had found the key to freeing both our worlds from the Order.

But over time and months, we'd realized that once Priestess Winter died, her four sisters had taken measures to make sure we wouldn't find them. So far, our search had been completely in vain and we were no closer to destroying them than we were in the beginning.

Our lives had settled into a peaceful routine here in Peachville, but the coming battles were never far from our minds.

As I walked through the ruins of the old gate, I found a piece of the statue that had once held my brother's spirit trapped inside while the town waited for its Prima to come home. I sat down beside it and pulled out the memory stone again, then let my thoughts drift back to the day this gate had first opened over a hundred years ago.

The day the Order of Shadows ripped my brother from my life.

BROKEN
THE SHADOW WORLD, 101 YEARS AGO

*L*EA'S LIPS TOUCHED mine, not out of passion but out of desperation.

The veil surrounding us lifted and a gasp rushed through the crowd.

I tried to lift myself from the ground, but my legs were too weak to hold me. Lea gripped my hand as her father came rushing forward off the throne.

"What is it?" he asked.

"It's Aerden," she said, low so the crowd couldn't hear. "Something horrible's happened."

My father appeared at my side, his face stricken with panic. I had never in my life seen him lose control or show emotion. He was a rock, always accepting fate as it came to him.

But that day, in that brief moment in the throne room, I saw a side to my father I never knew existed.

"We must get him out of here," he said. He lifted me from Lea's grasp and shifted, soaring through the air so fast it turned my stomach.

Behind us in the hall, there was shouting and movement as the crowd tried to understand what was happening.

"I don't understand," someone said before the door to the king's chambers had closed. "Did they kiss?"

My father set me down on a stone bench near the wall and I leaned over, retching.

I felt as if I had fallen from a great height with no ability to fly or shift. Having Aerden's presence taken from me was like hitting the ground at full speed. My muscles were sore and weak and my connection to my magic felt distant. Broken.

"What's happening to me?" I asked.

My father paced the floor beside me. For the moment, we were alone in the chamber room. "Did you have a vision? You must tell me what you saw."

I tried to sit up and he rushed to my side, helping to prop me against the wall.

I closed my eyes and took several deep breaths, each one hurting more than the last. I winced in pain, then shook my head. "I don't think it was a vision," I said. "This was different."

"Different how?"

"It wasn't like being pulled into a picture of the future," I explained, trying to remember exactly what I'd seen and felt. "I still saw images of him in my head, the same as when I have visions, but this time, I felt him. It was almost like I was standing by his side, watching it happen. I could hear him, father. It's never been like that before."

My father turned his back to me and lowered his head.

I wanted to tell him more, if only to try to make sense of it in my head, but the chamber door burst open. Lea and her parents walked in, followed by my mother. A maidservant bowed and left the room, shutting the door behind her.

Lea rushed straight to my side and knelt at my feet. She rested her head against my leg and reached up to take my hand. "Are you okay?" she whispered.

I didn't have an answer. Was I okay? Would I ever be okay?

"Tell us exactly what happened," the king commanded.

The small group in the room formed a circle around Lea and I.

Pain surged through me and I clutched my side. How could I explain to them what I had experienced when I didn't even understand it myself?

I nearly lost consciousness, but Lea's hand on mine held me to this moment.

"Aerden and I have always had a bond," I said. I pushed through the pain, but my voice was strained and rough against my throat. "Even when we're separated, I have always been able to reach out to him with my mind and my magic."

My vision blurred and I let my head fall back against the cool glass wall.

"He's ill, can't you see that?" Lea said, standing and placing herself between her parents and me. "He needs rest and a shaman, not questions."

"It is not your place to give me orders," the king said. His voice echoed through the chamber room. "Now, stand aside."

Lea lifted her chin, but sat down as she was told.

I reached for her hand and she clasped it tight.

"This morning, I went looking for Aerden and he was gone," I said. "I can't tell you why he left, but it unsettled me the rest of the day."

"Did you know about this?" the king asked my father.

He nodded. "Yes, we knew Aerden was gone, but he had left of his own will."

I studied my father. I couldn't help but feel there was an undertone of secrecy in his voice. What was he keeping from me?

"Go on," the king said, looking to me.

"Throughout the ceremony, I couldn't stop thinking of him," I said. I paused as pain pulsed through my chest. "I couldn't help but feel something was wrong, so I reached out with my magic like I'd done a million times before."

"And you found him?" my mother asked, bringing a trembling hand to her mouth.

I met her eyes and shook my head. "Not at first," I said. "I wondered if maybe he had gotten too far away, beyond the reach of my bond with him. It had never happened before, but we hadn't really ever tested it."

Lea stroked my arm and having her by my side made this moment both worse and better at the same time. I was glad to have her support when I was being questioned this way. But at the same time, with her there, I couldn't be completely honest, either.

"But then, when we were inside the veil, exchanging our stones, I felt him appear at the edge of my awareness," I said. I couldn't tell them why I was thinking of him when Lea touched her stone, so I pushed slightly beyond the boundaries of the truth. "I think he was reaching out to me, to tell me he was in trouble."

"What did you see?"

"I saw my brother," I said, the vision of him in chains bringing new pain to the surface. I tightened my jaw, anger and agony running through my body. "He was shackled and bleeding, kneeling in a field of black roses."

Lea's mother gasped and turned away. The king's head snapped toward his wife, but the look on his face was one of warning rather than comfort. It struck me as odd, and I wondered if I was wrong to tell them everything I had seen. I felt separated from them, as if they were keeping a great secret.

But I had to tell them. If they knew more than they were telling me, then they were our best hope for finding Aerden's killers and bringing them to justice.

"Some kind of bright light hovered in the air in front of him. It was almost like a shimmering waterfall, but it was oval and perfectly formed," I said.

"An emerald light?" my mother asked. She clutched her robes in her fists.

I met her eyes. She definitely knew something about this light. I could see it in her face. In all their faces.

"No," I said, not taking my eyes from her. "A sapphire blue light, as bright and clear as the garden of lillies in your back yard."

She swallowed, her lips trembling, betraying the importance of the light. She turned to my father, her eyes filled with rage and terror.

He held his palm up, silencing her before she had a chance to say another word.

The others stood stone-still. I saw fear in their eyes. Even the eyes of the King of the North.

"What else?" my father asked when he'd found his voice again.

"A woman," I said. "I couldn't see her face or her form. She wore a hood of blue velvet over her head. She appeared inside the portal. Then, a flash of something that looked like the insignia of a dragon on a man's coat. That was when Aerden seemed to look straight at me. He said my name and then he was just gone."

I lowered my head, tears flowing from somewhere deep inside my soul. The pain and regret in my brother's voice would haunt me forever.

"That's how I knew this wasn't a vision of the future," I said. "Because he knew I was there with him. He was trying to tell me something, but he never got the chance. Whoever they were, they killed him. I felt him ripped from me as if he'd been cut from my own flesh."

I cried out and struggled to my feet. I wanted to ask them what they knew. I wanted to demand the truth from them all.

But the moment I stood, a darkness washed over me. I fell to the marble floor, unable to control the seizure that hammered its way through my body.

When it stopped, my mother's face appeared above me, stained with tears and lined with worry. She stroked my forehead, then lifted her eyes to my father.

"It was them, wasn't it?" she asked him. "What have we done?"

That was the last thing I heard before the pain dragged me under its dark curtain.

IF GIVEN A CHOICE

When I awoke, Lea was sitting by my side. Her head rested against the blanket covering my legs and her hand lay stretched out toward mine.

I tried to swallow, but my throat was dry and cracked. My tongue seemed to be permanently stuck to the roof of my mouth.

I lifted my head, pushing up on the bed with my arms. Some of my strength had returned, but I still felt less. Diminished, somehow. Would I ever be whole again? Or would I spend the rest of my life as half of a demon, eternally missing my brother's presence at my side?

Lea woke, her dark eyes searching mine.

Her lower lip trembled and she reached for my hand. "Denaer, how are you feeling?"

An impossible question. "I feel broken," I said, my voice rough as the rocky shore of the Sea of Glass.

Lea stood and walked to a cart that held water, cheese, fruit and breads that smelled freshly made. She poured a glass of water and brought it to me. "Here, this will help," she said.

I drank it down, then asked for more.

"How long have I been asleep?" I cursed myself for being too weak to stay conscious. With every moment that passed, Aerden's killer had a chance to get farther away. We couldn't let the trail go cold. We had to find that field of black roses and search for any clues that might have been left behind.

Lea handed me a fresh glass of water. She pressed her lips together and furrowed her brow.

"It's been two weeks," she said, sinking back down into the chair by the bed.

I sat up with a jerk, then immediately regretted it. The sore muscles on my side burned as if they'd been ripped open and held to a flame.

Lea placed her hands on my shoulders and gently pushed me back against the pillows. "It's going to take time," she said. "You have to be patient."

"What's happening to me?" I asked.

She shook her head. "They aren't sure," she said. "We've had three shamans in to examine you, but they can't seem to find anything physically wrong with you except that your aura is weak. In meditation, father's shaman could sense a rip down the left side of your power, as if—"

"As if a piece of myself had been ripped from my body." I already knew. I felt it the moment my brother was taken from me.

"I'm so sorry," she said. She lifted my hand toward her face and nuzzled her cheek against my knuckles.

I pulled away.

I didn't deserve her affections. If it had been Aerden standing inside the veil with her, he never would have died. Instead, I took his sacrifice and passed it off as my own truth while he was being tortured.

I would never forgive myself.

Hurt registered on Lea's face, but she recovered quickly, standing and pacing the floor beside my bed.

"Your parents will want to know you're awake," she said. "Do you want me to go get them?"

I looked around for the first time since I'd regained consciousness. Instead of my own room, I was in a room I didn't recognize. The walls here were adorned with strips of gold woven together in an intricate pattern. The fabrics were lush and heavy in colors like deep navy and burgundy.

"Where am I?" I asked. "Are we in the castle?"

"Yes," she said. Her hand fluttered to the golden locket she now wore on a long chain around her neck. "Your home is here now that we are officially promised to each other."

I brought my hand to my lips. Our kiss hadn't been mutual, but all the veil needed was a kiss.

And now I was promised to a princess I didn't love.

But I had also made a promise to my brother. I told him I would never hurt Lea. I promised that she would never know the truth about the stone I gave to her.

I held my hand out to her and she walked toward me. She placed her small hand inside mine and I slowly brought it to my lips, tears welling up in my eyes.

"Lea," I said.

"Yes?" she whispered.

"Can I trust you?" I asked.

She drew her eyebrows together and tilted her head to the side. "Of course," she said. "Why are you asking me that?"

I pushed myself up again, wincing slightly at the pain, but learning now to ignore it and move beyond it. I had no time for rest. I'd already lost way too much time as it was.

"Because I need to know that if given a choice of loyalty, you would choose me above all others," I said. I knew I was asking too much of her. I knew it was wrong when she believed my love for her ran deeper than it did, but I needed her. She was all I had in this world. "I need to know that you would never betray me. Not even if the king himself asked you to."

My heart thrummed in my ears.

Her lips parted and she sucked in a deep breath. She raised a hand again to her locket, closing her fist around it.

Finally, she nodded. "I am yours now," she said. "I would die for you if you asked me to. And I will never, ever betray you."

I kissed her hand again, then leaned back against the pillows, worn out from even such small exertions.

Guilt pierced through my chest.

Would she have given so much of herself and been willing to make such sacrifices if she had known the truth?

But it was too late to worry about things like that. Aerden was gone and even those we should have trusted most knew more than they were willing to admit. I was determined to reveal their secrets and find the truth about what happened to my brother.

And someday, whoever took him would pay for what they had done.

I would never rest until that day came.

THIS WON'T BRING HIM BACK

*N*O MATTER HOW many times I questioned my parents, they insisted they knew nothing about what happened to Aerden or who would have wanted to hurt him.

They claimed the king had dispatched a group of guards to investigate the murder, but that so far, no one had found any evidence of who might have taken him.

Months passed with no answers, and every time I asked about the guards' progress, I was given a vague answer with no concrete details.

Lea and I spent hours going through maps of the Northern Kingdom, searching for any mention of black roses. Even in the older maps, we couldn't find anything promising.

The search for Aerden's killer ruled my days and nightmares of his death ruled my nights.

Always, he was kneeling across the thorns, crying out for me.

Some nights, I could feel the silver shackles cutting into my wrists. They were real to me and when I woke my wrists would be sore and red, as if my nightmares were taking over my life. The only way I could shake them was to draw exactly what I saw.

I'd never been interested in art or drawing, but I found that it helped me to get my memories and my visions on paper.

Sometimes, I stayed up several days in a row working to perfect a single image. I couldn't rest until every single detail was exactly the way I'd seen it in my mind. What if something that seemed insignificant turned out to be the key to it all? So I learned to pay attention to my visions in a new way. I learned to see the entire picture, piece by piece, and hold it there in my mind until I could get it on paper.

Years went by like this.

When we'd been through all of the maps, I started going from village to village with my drawings in hand, asking for any information on black roses, a silver dagger with blue stones, a woman in blue velvet robes with intricately woven patterns of silver. A red dragon. No one would talk to me.

After ten years, I was beginning to lose hope.

"Someone has to know something," I said to Lea one day on our way home from the village of Baurmon. "Aerden hadn't been gone long when he was taken. He could only have gone so far away in that short of time. Someone within that radius around the city has to know where there is a field of black roses. They are too rare to miss."

"I don't know." She sighed. "We've been over this a thousand times. What if we never find the answers?"

I snapped my head toward her. "Don't say that. It's only been ten years. We have an eternity to find answers."

She closed her eyes and swallowed. "We cannot spend the rest of our days tirelessly searching for answers," she said. She placed her hand on my arm. "This won't bring him back."

I yanked my arm from her touch, my jaw tense. "It isn't about bringing him back," I said.

"Then what is it about?"

"Do you really have to ask me that?" I pushed up the sleeves of my long coat. "You don't know me at all."

Lea lifted her chin. "I know this is all you think about," she said. "You're obsessed to the point of losing yourself, Denaer."

I turned away from her, but she stepped behind me, gripping my arm.

"We've been engaged for ten years and not once have we talked about our future," she said. "You don't kiss me or hold me or dream of having a child with me. You don't even talk about what it will be like someday to rule this kingdom. All you do is talk about a brother who is gone and never coming back."

I shifted into black smoke, pulling away from her grasp and reforming several steps away. "He was my twin. He was a piece of me," I said. "It's my duty to avenge his death, but I can't do that until I can find the demon who took his life. After ten long years, we are no closer to finding the truth and yes, it eats at me to the point of obsession. It lives with me every second of every day, and I will not let it go. Not until I know the truth. So don't ask me to dream of some future happiness when I am missing half of my own soul."

She lowered her chin to her chest and touched her hand to her forehead. "I want answers, too," she said. "I loved him as a brother, too. But we have to learn to move forward. I know you loved him, but you love me, too. And I need to know that there's a future for us beyond this search. Can't our love be enough?"

She looked up, her green eyes shimmering with tears.

I pressed my lips together to keep them from trembling. Sorrow and guilt pinched the back of my throat. "No," I said. "It will never be enough."

Lea's breath hitched and she clamped her hand to her mouth, then shifted into black smoke.

I clenched my fists and let my head fall back. I didn't mean to let that slip out, but she was pushing me too hard.

I had to follow her.

She had left the main road and flown into a dark wooded area. I followed the trail of her magic, flying fast through the trees to catch up to her. The forest was dense and dark with gnarled trees that split off in many directions, and I had to force my focus onto her trail, blocking out everything on either side.

And when the trail broke through the barrier of trees and into a clearing, I stopped, finding her staring out into a field.

"I'm sorry, Lea," I said. "I shouldn't have—"

"Shut up," she said, gripping my chin between her thumb and index finger.

I stepped back in shock. She'd never spoken to me so firmly. I didn't understand until she turned my head to the side, forcing me to really look at the clearing here in the middle of the dark forest.

I gasped and fell to my knees.

Spread out before us were more than a thousand black roses.

A RED DRAGON

THE PATTERN HERE wasn't the same circular pattern as what I'd seen in my vision, but this was the first real break we'd had in ten years.

Lea leaned down to touch one, but a voice spoke from the darkness just inside the trees to our left.

"You don't want to touch that," he said.

Lea stood and I moved in front of her, my hand out to the side to shield her. These roses were well hidden. Anyone who knew about them was likely partnered with whoever killed my brother.

My free hand went to the sword strapped to my back. Out of the corner of my eye, I saw Lea reach for her bow and arrow.

"Show yourself," I said.

Laughter sounded from the darkness.

"I'm not your enemy," the voice said.

A figure emerged from the cover of the gnarled trees. He was hovering in an in-between state, half shadow, half solid form. For him to hold onto both so steadily, he had to have tremendous amount of control and power.

He was tall and straight, his confidence obvious from the way he carried himself. He lifted his hands into the air, black shadows swirling around them.

"Who are you?" I asked. Every part of my body was on high alert, ready to react at any sudden movement or attack. Aerden had been one of the best warriors I'd ever known. For someone to have gotten the upper hand, they had to have been strong. Or very smart.

He did not answer.

He took several more steps toward us, keeping to the edge of the sinister flowers. His eyes moved beyond me and he lowered his eyes, bowing slightly at the waist. "Princess."

Behind me, Lea lowered her bow.

So he recognized us. Or at least her. Did that mean he was just a citizen of the city or one of the nearby villages? If so, what was he doing here by the roses?

"How did you come by these flowers?" I asked. "What do you know about them?"

He glanced toward the roses, an eyebrow raised. "I grew up in a village near here," he said. "My mother is an herbalist, making potions from plants and roots. She taught me a few things here and there."

"No one in the villages near here knows anything about these roses," I said. I didn't trust this demon.

"Well, that's because these are my roses," he said. He took several more steps toward us, and I didn't know whether to stand my ground or back away.

If these were his roses, then he definitely had some kind of connection to my brother's death. I just hadn't decided yet if he was friend or foe. There was something about his confidence that made me feel uneasy, as if I was being handled and manipulated.

He took another step and I pushed my sword out toward him. "You can stop there," I said.

He smiled and shrugged, lowering his hands. And when he did, a band around his arm came into clear view among the swirling shadows.

My heart stopped beating and the vision of Aerden's last moments came back to me in a rush. Someone wearing the same insignia had run toward him, but they had been cloaked in darkness.

Cloaked in shadows.

This demon wore the same insignia on a band around his arm.

A red dragon.

He was there when my brother died. I lifted my sword to his neck, my hands gripping the hilt so tightly my palms burned.

"You were there," I said, my voice strained in fury. "Speak, demon."

He stared at the sword, then raised his hands again and backed away. "I don't know what you're talking about," he said.

"Liar." I nodded toward his armband. "The dragon you wear on your arm. I've seen that before."

He glanced at his arm, then tilted his head and narrowed his eyes at me.

"Where?"

I took one hand off of my sword, but left the weapon outstretched toward him. I lowered my pack to the ground and dug through it until I found the right drawing. I shoved it toward him, then backed up again.

The demon gripped the page, his nostrils flaring. "Where did you get this?"

"I drew it," I said. "Do you deny that this is you?"

He studied the page harder. He brought the page up close to his eyes, taking his time looking at every single detail. This was my best drawing of the dragon, but I had enlarged it so that you couldn't see much of what else was going on in the background.

"This isn't me," he said.

"You're lying," I said. "The band is exactly the same. If it isn't you, then you surely know who it is. And I want answers."

"Answers about what?" he asked.

"About my brother's death," I said. This time, I was the one who stepped forward. I'd had it with this demon's conversation. He either needed to start giving clear answers or he needed to die.

After ten years of searching for something—anything—I was ready for blood.

"Tell me what you know, or so help me, you will die by this sword today."

The demon's eyes flicked toward Lea and he shook his head. "You would be wise to move on now," he said. "I can't help you."

I shifted and reformed behind him before he had a chance to move. My arm slipped around his throat and I pressed the tip of my sword against his side. I moved my mouth close to his ear, my teeth clenched tight. "What did you do?" I asked. "I need answers. Why Aerden? What did he do to deserve death at the hands of a demon like you?"

He didn't struggle against my hold. He didn't even seem concerned with my anger, which only further fueled my rage.

"Your brother?" he asked. "He's..."

He shook his head and shifted into shadows, slipping through my grasp like air. With the sword pressed against him as hard as I had it, he shouldn't have been able to shift completely into shadow form, but his ability to focus continued to surprise me.

"He's what?" I asked. The more he talked in circles, the more I wanted to see him kneeling at my feet, begging for mercy.

He reformed beside Lea and I barreled toward him, gripping his armband in my fist. I ripped it from his coat and shoved it in his face.

"What were you doing there when he died? I have to know," I said.

He didn't speak or even seem rattled by my anger. He simply turned his back on me.

"Talk," I said. I pressed my sword against his back, pushing deep enough to draw blood. "Or I will kill you. I swear it."

The demon turned around, a strange gleam in his eyes.

"I'd like to see you try," he said.

A TRUE WARRIOR

*R*AGE FLOWED THROUGH me and ice frosted over the length of my sword.

The demon's eyes widened and he smiled, taunting me.

I clenched my jaw tight and spun around, putting the full force of my anger into my weapon as it sliced through the air. In the instant before I split him in half, the demon shifted into shadow and flew high into the air, leaving a trail of black smoke behind him.

I shifted and pushed up from the ground, chasing him. He reformed at the opposite side of the circle of roses, then reached out and with his bare hand, he stopped one of Lea's arrows just before it pierced his skin. He simply closed his fist around it as if it had been moving in slow motion.

The arrow disintegrated into ash and floated to the ground. The demon wiped his hand against his leg, completely unfazed. With a flick of his wrist, vines emerged from the forest and wrapped around Lea's hands and legs. She screamed.

"I can't shift. Denaer, run," she said. "He's too powerful. Get help."

The vines tightened against her wrists and ankles, then jerked her backward, trapping her against a tree.

I swung my sword over the top of my head, then pulled it forward, sinking it deep into the ground in front of me. The earth around the blade froze in an instant. A frozen circle spread out in layers, going through the flowers on one side and the trees on the other, ice popping and cracking as it crystallized.

It happened in an instant, but the demon acted faster than I could have imagined. He squatted down and placed his hand flat against the ground. My ice path stopped spreading, then rapidly melted.

My chest tightened and I focused my eyes on the demon's face.

"Who the hell are you?" I asked. I had never sparred with anyone so effortlessly powerful.

"My name is Andros," he said. He nodded his head. "Nice to meet you."

He seemed to think this was funny. He didn't think we were capable of hurting him in any way, but he didn't understand the full force of my despair and anger. I wouldn't stop until I had brought him to his knees.

I gripped the hilt of my sword and pulled it from the ground. I secured it into my backpack and with both hands now free, I held them out from my sides. I planted my feet firmly on the ground and lifted, drawing water up from several layers below the surface. A hole opened in the ground in front of me and water poured from it.

I reached forward and pulled thin rods of ice from the fountain one at a time. I threw them toward the demon as fast as I could. One direct hit and the ice would pierce straight through him. He would die in moments.

He managed to dodge all but the last one.

My heart leapt into my throat as I watched the final rod soar through the air toward his neck.

His eyes widened and for a moment, I thought I had him beat.

Then, he drew in a breath and blew outward with a great force. Flames erupted from his mouth and the ice evaporated, not even a drop of water left.

The flames singed my skin and I fell backward, lifting my arms to protect my face from the heat. I scrambled against the ground, panic seizing my body. I was in way over my head. I needed to run, but I couldn't leave Lea here. I reached for my sword, trying to calculate the distance to her from here and whether I could sever all four vines before the demon could stop me.

But before I even realized what was happening, he pressed a dagger to my throat.

I tried to shift, but he had me locked into form.

I struggled against his grip, crying out when the tip of his dagger pierced my skin.

He leaned forward, his breath hot against my ear. "You have spirit," he said. "With training you could be a true warrior like your brother."

"Don't you dare speak of him," I said.

"Your brother isn't dead," he whispered.

I kicked against the ground, but wasn't strong enough to pull myself from his grip. I grabbed his arm, sending what was left of my magic through my hands and into his body. He should have frozen like a statue, but instead, a tiny layer of ice frosted over his clothing, then melted in an instant.

"Kill me if you must," I said. "But don't tell me lies."

"It's not a lie."

"I saw him die," I said. "I felt him ripped from me."

The demon loosened his grip and I scrambled to my feet, my hands going to my new wound. It burned so deeply, I felt feverish and ill.

"Not dead," he said. "Merely taken from this world."

I shook my head, not believing him.

"Impossible," I said. "Portal magic has been dead for centuries. There's no way to leave this world."

"It's been rediscovered," he said. He sheathed his dagger in a strip of leather at his waist.

I charged him, but he shifted. I lost my balance and stumbled against a tree. I didn't have the power for this kind of fight anymore. Without Aerden, I was nothing. Weak and helpless.

Even after ten years, I was broken without him.

I leaned my head against the tree, my throat constricting and my eyes hot with anger.

"Why, then?" I asked. "Why did you take him?"

The demon appeared behind me and I braced myself for pain as he reached out. But instead of hurting me, he placed a comforting hand on my back. I looked up, confused.

Compassion softened his dark eyes.

"I told you, I am not your enemy," he said.

"Then why were you there on the day my brother was taken?" I asked.

"I didn't take your brother," he said. "But I know who did."

SHE'S MY FUTURE
THE HUMAN WORLD, PRESENT DAY

BEHIND ME, SOMETHING moved in the woods at the outer edge of the clearing.

I stood, expecting to see my brother. Instead, it was Lea who emerged from the darkness.

"What are you doing way out here?" she asked. She'd taken her hair down and it flowed like black silk down her back.

"Just thinking of the past," I said. "Do you remember the day we first met Andros?"

Lea smiled. "I remember he kicked our asses," she said. "He could have killed us both if he'd wanted."

I shook my head. "If it wasn't for him, I wonder if I ever would have found out the truth about what happened to Aerden," I said. "If you hadn't found those black roses—"

"You were never going to stop searching for the truth," she said, avoiding my eyes. "Even if you'd never met Andros that day. Losing your brother changed you. Once it happened, there was never any real path back to the demon I used to know. Believe me, I searched."

She said it with a laugh, but her pain was still obvious, even after all these years.

"I never meant to hurt you," I said, the golden locket heavy in my pocket.

Lea kicked at a cluster of crushed stones. "I know," she said.

But she didn't know. All this time, I had kept my promise to Aerden. I had never told Lea that the heart stone I gave her on the day of our engagement was not my truth.

It was his.

My truth belonged to someone else. My heart was destined for another. It always had been.

Lea turned and brushed at her cheeks. She was so tough and hard these days, but I knew better. I knew that once upon a time, she had been soft and beautiful and full of hope.

I felt partially responsible for how drastically she had changed in the past hundred years.

What would our life had been like if Aerden had never been taken? What would she have been like?

I sighed and reached into my pocket. I curled my fist around the golden case, rubbing its smooth surface between my fingers. There was something I'd been wanting to do for a while and now, I realized this was the moment.

It was time.

I had already been the cause of so much of her pain, I hated to hurt her again, but there was only one path to my future. And in order to move forward, I had to remove certain obstacles from my past.

According to demon tradition, I was still engaged to her. Her desperate kiss to lower the veil had been enough to secure our promise and as long as I held her heart stone, I also held her heart.

It was time I let her go.

It was time we both moved on, once and for all.

"I never really said thank you for everything you did for me back then," I said. "You were there for me when I thought I'd lost everything, and I know there's nothing I could ever do to repay you for that."

She turned toward me, her eyes gleaming with tears.

"I loved you," she said. She lowered her head and another tear escaped down her cheek. "I still love you."

I took my hand from my pocket and opened my palm flat. The golden locket gleamed in the moonlight. "I need you to let me go," I said.

She lifted her hand to her throat and took a slow breath.

"You're going to propose to her?" she asked, raising her chin and straightening her shoulders.

"I love her," I said. "She's my future."

She bit down on her lip and took several deep breaths before she finally reached out and took the golden locket from my outstretched hand. "And I'm your past."

"Yes," I said, guilt like a rope around my heart.

Lea reached around her neck and pulled a thin gold chain over her head. Hanging on the end of it was the matching locket I'd given her when we met inside the veil one hundred and one years ago this day.

She unclasped the chain and slid the locket off into her hand. She lifted it to her lips and kissed it gently, tears streaming down her face.

It had been decades since I'd seen her show such emotion and vulnerability. I hated that I was the cause of such a deep wound in her heart.

She held the locket out to me and when I reached for it, she placed her other hand on top of mine and held my gaze for one long moment. "I don't know if it was Aerden's disappearance or if it was just the way we both changed over time that made your love for me fade," she said. "But the greatest happiness of my life was looking into the light of this stone and seeing myself through your eyes."

I held her hand tight for a moment before letting go. I ached to explain the truth. I wanted to tell her that it wasn't her fault. I wanted to tell her that it was never my light inside that stone.

Instead, I had to hold the secret in my heart, letting her live with the pain of her beliefs.

But I'd held onto my guilt and my shame for long enough. I'd sacrificed everything to make up for my mistakes. I'd paid for the lies I told.

And I had suffered long enough.

I deserved happiness and now that my brother was free, there was only one thing in this world or the next that I wanted.

Harper.

And now, on the anniversary of the day I thought I'd lost everything, I was finally free to make her mine.

PART II

—To Brandy
Your friendship is a light in the darkness.

YET TO COME
THE HUMAN WORLD, PRESENT DAY

Brighton Manor buzzed with energy. Music poured from the open windows and more than twenty guests gathered in what used to be the formal living room.

Friends smiled as I passed, but I only had eyes for one person. I searched for her blond hair and dark eyes. I looked for the curve of her face and the graceful movements of her body. And when I finally saw her, standing at the edge of the makeshift dance floor, my heart skipped a beat deep inside my chest.

A smile spread across her face, lighting her up from the inside. Her light pushed through me, warming the cold feeling in my heart.

I'd spent most of my night locked in memories of the past. Memories almost too painful to revisit.

But if I was ever going to be absolutely sure of her love, I needed to show her my truest self. Harper needed to understand my worst, darkest moment.

If she could see that and still love me and want to spend her life with me, then I knew together we could face anything.

But if she saw the horror of my rage—my wrath—and turned away from me, I wouldn't blame her. I would be heartbroken for eternity, but I would understand.

I'd spent the past fifty years hating myself for what I'd done in anger. How could I be surprised if she hated me, too, after seeing for herself what I'd once been capable of?

She crossed toward me, an extra glass of punch in her hand.

"Where did you run off to?" she asked, handing me one of the cups. When I didn't answer, she frowned. "You've been distant tonight. Is something going on?"

I brushed my hand against the stone in my pocket.

"I've just got a lot on my mind tonight," I said. I put one arm around her waist and pulled her body close to mine. I lowered my lips to her hair and inhaled the scent of her shampoo. "I love you so much."

She pulled away and narrowed her eyes at me. "Are you sure everything's okay?"

I wanted to comfort her and tell her that everything would be fine, but how could I do that?

The future was more uncertain than ever. A war with the Order of Shadows was close. Closer than she knew. With her father gone, Harper would have to carry the pressures of an entire kingdom on her shoulders. New enemies would come forward soon, their sole mission to destroy us and everything we've built here and in the world beyond.

Even the past was still standing between us. A giant wall of sorrow and rage. I felt like I stood behind that wall, its height cutting me off from her love. I didn't deserve her, and I knew it.

"Jackson?" she asked. She set her punch down on the table near the door and lifted her soft palm to my face. Her brown eyes were filled with worry. "What is it? Have you seen something? Please, talk to me."

I covered her hand with my own, caressing her soft skin, then grabbing her hand tight.

"I have some things I still need to take care of tonight," I said. "Enjoy the party. I'll back in a little bit, I promise."

She shook her head, her eyes glistening. "Don't shut me out, again," she said. "You promised. If you're going through something, you need to talk to me about it. Whatever it is, we can face it together."

I leaned down and kissed her forehead. "I'm not shutting you out," I said. In fact, I was doing the opposite, but there was no way to explain that to her without telling her about the memory stone. And I wasn't ready to do that, yet. "I promise you, I'll tell you everything before the night is over. I just need a little bit more time."

I brought her hand to my lips. I kissed the soft space between her thumb and index finger, then turned her hand and kissed the pad of her palm.

Sadness washed over her face, but she smiled despite her fear. "I'm going to hold you to that," she said.

I knew it was hard for her to trust. She'd been betrayed so many times by the people who were closest to her. She'd opened herself up to people who abused her kindness and her desire to belong and to have friends. Hell, she'd even had to deal with my own betrayals. I had kept so much from her for so long. And even now, I had my secrets.

But despite all those past pains, Harper was putting her trust in me now. She would give me the space I needed to finish this tonight. And knowing how much that cost her—how much of her own heart she was willing to risk to make me happy—made me love her even more.

Made me deserve her even less.

I kissed her again, then turned and left the party.

I needed silence and solitude now to finish my walk through the past. Seeing my engagement to Lea would be hard for Harper, but nothing could be as awful as the years that followed.

I found a quiet spot in the garden and sat down at the edge of the fountain. I reached into my pocket and grasped the memory stone tightly in my fist, knowing the most painful part was yet to come.

THE TAKINGS

THE SHADOW WORLD, 90 YEARS AGO

I STARED AT THE demon with the red dragon on his armband. He had said Aerden was still alive. Could that be possible? All these years my mind had been turned toward vengeance. Not once did I dare to hope he could be alive.

"What do you know?" I asked. I tried to calm my heart. I didn't know this demon. He could easily be lying to me in an attempt to pull me into the same trap that ended my brother's life. I needed to keep my hope at arm's length.

"He doesn't know anything," Lea said, moving to stand between us. She rubbed her wrists. "Anyone who would dare to attack the daughter of the king is obviously a rebel. We would be smart to call in the sentinels to deal with this trash."

Andros smirked, one side of his face curling up into a strangely confident smile. "You truly are the daughter of the king," he said.

She narrowed her eyes at him and took a step forward. "What's that supposed to mean?"

He raised an eyebrow and shook his head. "Nothing, Princess," he said. "Only that you are perhaps as blind as your own father, refusing to see what is happening in your own kingdom."

I studied him. What was he trying to say? I had never heard anyone dare to say a rude word to Princess Lazalea. From the look on her face, she was barely holding on to her control. By all rights, she should have called in her father's guards and had Andros thrown in the dungeon for the way he had disrespected her.

But deep in my heart, I felt the twist of an ugly truth.

There was definitely something going on that the king refused to acknowledge. I'd known it since the moments after Aerden's death. In the king's chambers, he and my parents had shared secret looks and spoken of things beyond my understanding.

"Give me one reason why I shouldn't have you punished for speaking of me and my father this way?" Lea stood tall, her eyes dark and angry.

"Because, like I said, I know who took his brother," Andros said, his eyes flicking toward me. He shrugged. "I'm sure you've discovered by now that no one else is going to talk to you. They are too scared of what might happen if they tell the truth about what's been going on in the villages."

"What truth?" I demanded. "Stop speaking in secrets."

Andros held up his hands. "The villagers are scared to talk because the king has forbidden anyone to discuss the takings," he said. "What risk do I take upon myself if I talk directly to the king's daughter? You've already threatened to have me thrown into your castle's dungeons. If I tell you the truth, what assurances do I have that you will not turn me in to your father?"

"The takings?" I asked.

But he didn't answer. He kept his eyes trained on Lea's face, waiting for an answer. He wanted a promise that we wouldn't turn his words against him.

"What assurances do we have that you're even telling the truth?" she asked.

"If you promise not to turn your father's Sentinels on me, I will show you proof of what I know," he said. "Proof that there is a group, not of this world, who has been taking demons through portals to the other side."

"Taking them for what use?" My lip trembled as I asked the words. I struggled to keep my emotions in check. Could Aerden truly be alive? And if so, what torture was he being subjected to?

"We don't know," Andros said. "But if you guarantee my safety, I will tell you all that I know."

Lea backed toward me, shaking her head. "I don't think he's to be trusted," she said. "You said you saw an armband identical to his in your vision of the day Aerden was taken. How can we know he didn't kill your brother? How do we know he isn't trying to kill us, too? He did, after all, string me up with a set of very strong vines."

Her wrists were bruised from the rope-like vines that had held her captive. He was powerful, there was no doubt about that. Probably powerful enough to have defeated my brother. But Aerden had said it was a woman who had spoken with him. And I had seen a portal in my vision. Some kind of bright light with a hooded woman waiting inside.

"Tell me one thing in truth," I said to him. "Were you there when my brother was killed? Was it your armband I saw in my vision?"

Andros shook his head. "I was not there. I give you my word," he said. "But someone from my group was there on that day. A demon called Mirabi."

"I want to speak with him," I said.

"Impossible," he said. "My friend Mirabi died that day. Until now, I hadn't been certain how or why, but if he was there, he was trying to save your brother, not harm him. I promise you."

"He's lying," Lea said.

I held my hand up to silence her. Lea had always had such a quick temper. She had already judged this demon the moment he attacked her. But I attacked him first.

And something in his story rang true to me.

I needed to see this proof he was offering.

"If we promise our silence, when can we see this proof you spoke of?"

"Two nights from now," he said. "Meet me here in the forest. I will show you."

I nodded. "You have our promise," I said.

Lea opened her mouth to protest, but I met her eyes, begging. Her mouth snapped shut and she crossed her arms in front of her chest and turned away.

When I turned back toward Andros to agree to his terms, he was gone, leaving only a thin trail of black smoke in his wake.

I HAD TO KNOW

LEA AND I barely spoke on the walk back to the gates of the city. I couldn't stop thinking about Andros. I'd never met another demon like him in my life. He wasn't afraid to say it like it was, and he wasn't afraid to speak against the king. Even to the king's daughter.

But how could I be sure he was trustworthy? How could I know he wasn't trying to trap or trick me in some way?

Still, I knew I had to see his proof. I had to know.

Over the years since Aerden died, I'd nearly gone insane from the lack of answers and information. I was convinced my parents knew more than they were saying, and I'd suspected the same was true of many of the villagers I'd spoken to. What were they all so afraid of?

What were they hiding?

If there was even the slightest chance Andros had the answers, I had to see this through.

And if there was a chance my brother was alive...

I was terrified to even allow myself to think it, but the seed of hope had already been planted. After believing I was doomed to an eternity without him, my heart ached for the possibility of seeing him again. If there was any chance Aerden was still alive, I had to see this through. No matter the cost.

"We should talk to our parents," Lea said the next morning over breakfast.

Now that we were officially promised to each other, we were free to come and go in each other's quarters as often as we wanted. Right now, that was both a blessing and a curse. Lea wanted so much more from me than I could give, and after she'd seen the strong love inside the heart stone, she believed I cared for her so much more than I truly did.

It was Aerden's love she saw, not mine. It had been his final sacrifice to protect her happiness and my honor.

Only, honor didn't seem quite as important anymore. Not considering the depth of the sacrifices we'd all had to make. Honesty seemed more honorable now, but I didn't have the courage to tell her the truth. Instead, like a coward, I kept up the lie that I knew would eventually tear her apart.

"I don't think it's a good idea," I said. I didn't want to get into an argument with her first thing in the morning, but I had a feeling it was unavoidable. I wasn't going to back down on this. "Not until we have more concrete answers."

She shook her head and stood up from the small table in my outer chambers. She walked over toward the balcony. A gentle wind blew through the archway, lifting her long black hair up from her neck.

"We can't do this alone," she said. "If Andros is right and someone has actually taken your brother through some portal, we'll need to act fast. We'll need an army to go in there and get him. No one is better equipped to deal with this or to fight back than my father. We should go to him."

"No," I said. I pushed my plate of fruit and pastries to the side. I had no appetite these days. "Don't you see? If we have no proof other than some rebel who lives outside of the city; our parents and the council will all tell us we're reaching for something that isn't there. They'll tell us it's nonsense and insist we look no further. Then we'll be trapped. We won't be able to even investigate the truth without directly disobeying the crown."

"So you're saying we should go behind everyone's back, risking Aerden's life in the process?"

"It's riskier for him if we go to the king and he doesn't believe us," I said. "We need proof. Or at least some kind of solid evidence that will convince them we're on the right track. Andros says he has that. Once we've seen whatever it is he's going to show us, we can talk about the next step."

Lea turned to me, sadness etched across her dark features. "What if he's just gone?" she asked. "What if this demon has no idea what he's talking about? What if he's wrong about Aerden and you spend the rest of your days searching for a ghost?"

I turned away from her, not wanting to hear this. She'd been with me every step of my search so far, but lately, she'd been mentioning our future more and more. She was ready to move on.

But how could she ask that of me? Especially now, after all that Andros had said?

"If there's any hope he's alive, I'll search for as long as it takes," I said. "I won't abandon my brother."

She moved toward me, placing a gentle hand on my arm.

"I'm not asking you to abandon him," she said. "I'm just asking you to open your mind to the possibility that he's gone and he's never coming back. Maybe there's nothing you can do to help him, because his light has gone out."

"If that's true, then I need to understand how. Why. I need to know who did this to him," I said. *And I need to make them pay.*

"Ten years," she said, pulling away. "We've been looking for answers for ten years and we're no closer to the truth after all this time. No one will talk, Denaer. No one will tell us what they know, if anyone knows anything."

"Andros knows," I said.

"Andros is a wildcard," she said. "A rebel. He works and lives with those who would betray my father and my family in order to gain power. We can't trust anything he says. He may have ulterior motives for turning us against my father."

"I agree that we should move forward very carefully when it comes to Andros, but I still need to know what he knows," I said. "This is the first real lead we've had since Aerden disappeared. You can't ask me to walk away from that."

She sighed and leaned against the pillar, looking out onto the streets of the king's city. After a moment, she turned back to me, her green eyes dark and stormy. "Promise me you'll go into this with your eyes open."

"My eyes are wide open," I said.

"Open to the past," she whispered. She took my hand in hers and pressed it against her lips. "But what about the future?"

The look in her eyes made my stomach tense. I turned away, unable to meet her gaze. I knew she wanted me to comfort her and tell her that our future was something I dreamed about, but I didn't have the energy to lie to her right now.

The truth was that a future without Aerden meant nothing to me.

THEY ALREADY KNEW

A VOICE STOPPED ME in the hallway of the castle. My mother.

I hesitated, then turned back toward her. We used to be so close, as a family, but I knew she was hiding something from me. Every time she lied and said she knew nothing more about Aerden's disappearance, I felt us moving farther apart.

"Where are you headed in such a rush? And at this hour?" she asked.

"I'm meeting a friend."

"It's nearly nightfall," she said, her face wrinkled.

I didn't offer any more information and she didn't ask again. Over the past few years, I'd learned it was better to be vague and give very few details about my life. I already knew she didn't approve of the way I'd continued to search for answers.

In the early days after Aerden had disappeared, I went to my parents with every single tiny shred of evidence about who might have wanted to hurt him. Even the tiniest clue was something I wanted to discuss with them. I wanted to hear their feedback and see what they had to say or if they'd heard anything. I didn't understand why they weren't out there searching with me. Why didn't they need answers like I did?

After a few years, it started to sink in that my parents had no interest in finding out the truth.

In fact, they began to get upset with me for continuing to ask questions.

"Let him go," they'd said a thousand times. "Your life is with Lea now."

Their words burned me to the core. How could they ask me to let him go? And how could they forget him so easily?

Any time I tried to question my father's lack of emotion over losing his son, he said he only wanted to be strong for my mother. He said that she had been unable to grieve and move on because of my constant questions. He'd said we all needed to let Aerden live on in our hearts and memory but to move on with our lives. He told me that's what Aerden would have wanted.

But instead of quieting my search and letting my brother's memory rest, my father's blindness only made me angry.

He should have been by my side searching for the demon who had killed Aerden. They both should have.

It had always bothered me that my parents kept pushing me to put Aerden's disappearance behind us.

But after hearing what Andros had to say, I wondered how I could have been so blind all this time.

The reason they weren't searching for the truth was that they already knew the truth.

Their questions and anger had nothing to do with my mother's ability to grieve and everything to do with the fact that they did not want me to find the real truth. There was something important they didn't want me to know, and they would stop at nothing to make sure I never found out.

"Who are you meeting?" she asked.

"Lea," I said, which was true.

Her eyes narrowed into dark slits. "And who else?"

I swallowed. "Why do you need to know?

I was tired of her questions. Her constant lies. I would never forgive her if I discovered Aerden was still alive and she knew about it. My anger would know no limits. I could feel it growing inside me even now.

"Denaer, there are those out there who would see you fall into madness," she said. She moved toward me and put her hand on my cheek. I pulled away and she frowned. "Be careful of the lies those people would tell in order to manipulate you, son. You are the future ruler of this kingdom. That comes with a great deal of responsibility. I hope you understand that. There are dangers out there you can't possibly understand."

I gave no answer, but I understood. Yes, there were those who would use me for their own personal gain, not the least of whom was standing right in front of me.

"Will you be back before nightfall?" she asked.

I gave her a quick bow. "Not likely," I said, then turned and shifted into black smoke. I didn't give her the chance to ask anything more of me, and by the time night did fall, I was nowhere near the castle walls.

THE DEEPEST KIND OF DARKNESS

*A*NDROS WAS WAITING for us by the roses.
He didn't see us at first, so I stood there for a moment watching him through the darkness.

He leaned down at the edge of a small patch of flowers and closed his eyes. He lifted his hand over the flowers and mumbled something I couldn't quite make out.

A bluish black mist of energy rose up from the flowers like a fog, flowing into the demon's hand. Then, Andros cried out and yanked his hand backward, falling onto his back.

I rushed over toward him.

"Are you okay?" I asked.

He cradled his hand close to his chest. "I'm fine," he said, laughing. "Just one of the dangers of experimentation, I guess."

"What were you trying to do?" Lea asked.

"Honestly?"

I nodded.

He shook his head and laughed. "I have no idea."

"What was the black fog that rose up from them?" Lea asked. "Where did it come from?"

"I haven't completely figured it out yet, but these roses have some kind of property that allows them to pull energy from the magic around them," he said. He lifted his hand over the cluster of black roses and moved it in a circle. I could instantly feel the energy of his magic as it entered the air, and within a few seconds, I could physically see it too. "Watch this."

I watched as the energy field of his magic transferred from his hands to the tips of the roses. It was as if the roses were a magnet, drawing the energy toward them.

The dark black smoke of his power drifted toward the roses and hovered above it.

"Now what?" I asked. "Does the magic get absorbed into the flowers?"

Andros shook his head and moved his hand away from the roses. The smoke hovered for a moment, then gradually faded altogether.

"It doesn't seem to actually soak in," he said. "The roses attract the power, but they don't seem to have a way to store it. They appear to be more of a conductor of energy. It's hard to understand, but that's why I started growing them here. I want to understand them. I think they're important."

"I've seen these roses before," I said, looking out over the darkened field. The light of the moons was dim tonight, but I had always been able to see very clearly in the dark. It was one of my gifts. "The day my brother disappeared, I got a very strong vision of him. He was kneeling in a circle of these roses, bleeding and crying out. There was a bright light shining inside the circle."

I struggled with the memory. It was difficult to talk about it, even now.

"Tonight may prove to be a very emotional one for you, my friend, but I think you are on the verge of finding answers to questions you have held for a very long time," he said.

"Where are you taking us?" Lea asked.

She was still unsure about us being here, and I knew it was a lot to ask of her. If the king found out we were meeting with rebels, he would be very unhappy. I knew she was only here out of loyalty to me, which only deepened my guilt.

"You'll see very soon," Andros said.

"What do the roses have to do with what happened to my brother?" I asked. "I know the two things are tied together. It's the only real clue I've had to follow."

Andros looked across the field of black, his eyes growing darker and more distant, as if he was remembering some great pain. "That's where information gets complicated," he said. "And privileged. I'm taking a very big risk showing you these things."

"I need to know."

"Once you've seen what I'm about to show you, you'll never be able to go back to life the way it was before," Andros said. He looked from me to Lea, meeting our eyes. "It will change everything. Are you sure you're ready for this kind of truth?"

"My world has already been changed forever," I said. "The moment my twin brother was torn from me, it was like I went over some kind of cliff. I fell into the deepest kind of darkness. How could my life ever be the same after that?" I shook my head and ran a hand through my hair. "I'm going to follow this path as far as it goes, and believe me when I say that whoever is responsible for this is going to pay for what they've done. It's the one thing I can say with complete confidence. I won't rest until they've paid for this with their life."

Andros lifted and eyebrow and laughed. "You sound like one of us."

"Who's us?" Lea asked.

He ran a hand across his cheek, studying her. "The Resistance," he said. "It's a small group for now, but it's growing."

"What are you resisting, exactly?" she asked. Her tone was biting. Untrusting.

"You really are sheltered, aren't you?"

Andros walked toward a black bag lying on the ground. He picked it up and slung it over his shoulder, a look of amusement on his face.

"What's that supposed to mean?"

"I mean, how is it possible you've never heard of The Resistance?" he said. "Only someone who'd been sheltered deep within the castle walls could be so blind to what's been going on in the outerlands."

A hollow feeling took over in my stomach. "Yes, we've been sheltered," I said. "But I'm here to find out the truth."

Andros paused and turned around. "And what about you, Princess?" he asked. "Are you ready to find out the truth? Even if it means finding out that your father is not as honorable as you think he is?"

Lea's jaw tensed and her hands clenched into tight fists at her side. "I'm here to take a look at the facts with open eyes and make up my own mind about what's real and what isn't," she said.

Andros made a face. "Inviting you into my world and sharing my knowledge with you is either the smartest thing I've ever done," he said. "Or the dumbest. But if the two of you are to be our leaders someday, I think you have a right to know what's going on. I think you have a right to see what your king has worked so hard to keep hidden from you and the rest of the citizens inside his precious, gated, city of gold."

His voice trailed off and he looked out across the roses again.

Finally, he squinted up at the moons shining above.

"Come," he said. "It's time."

DARK PURPOSE

ANDROS SHIFTED TO pure black smoke and I knew the time for questions was gone. It was now or never.

I looked to Lea, making sure she was truly ready to follow where this would lead. She gave me a sad smile, then shifted and followed the trail of smoke Andros had left behind.

I followed them through the dark forest, then out across a field of firegrass that sparked across the backdrop of the night sky. We came across a worn path and followed it for a long while, then suddenly split off from the road and cut through another dark forest full of thorned trees and nightwhispers.

I could barely keep up with them. Without my night vision, they would have lost me miles ago. I had no idea how Lea was following him with such ease, but I was impressed. And jealous.

When we broke through the trees, the Sea of Glass stared back at us, the moons' glow dancing on the black surface of the water. True to its name tonight, it was as still and motionless as glass.

We followed the shoreline toward a cluster of lights in the distance.

Klashok. I recognized this village.

I had been here once when my father took Aerden and me fishing as children. We had hired a guide who took us on his boat across the sea. We'd spent the day casting nets out into the clear water. Aerden had caught a large spiderfish and I had caught a whestler. It had been a very good day.

Even from this distance, I could tell the town had changed. The homes on the outskirts were practically in ruins. Abandoned, by the looks of it.

There used to be a large, sturdy pier leading out into the water nearly a mile, with boats lined up as far as the eye could see, but part of it had collapsed into the sea.

"What happened here?" I whispered when we stopped just outside the village.

A young girl appeared beside me out of nowhere. "This is what's happening all around," she said, her voice so low I almost couldn't hear her at all. "The villages that have been hit the hardest are falling into such horrible poverty they can't afford to replace and repair the older buildings and structures that have stood for centuries. Many of the elders have been taken, leaving no one to pass their power on to the village. It's devastating."

I wanted to ask her more and find out who she was and where she had come from, but Andros motioned for us to be quiet.

He crouched low and shifted, his smoke slithering inland, away from the shore and out into a large field of firegrass on the other side of the village.

We followed quietly. I noticed several others had joined our small group. Members of The Resistance, I'd guessed.

My pulse raced as we moved into the grass. What would we find here? What exactly was he going to show me?

The girl had said elders had been taken. Did that mean they were taken by the same people who took my brother? I was anxious for answers, but afraid of what truth lay beyond this moment.

Firegrass can grow very tall if left untended and this particular field was almost tall enough to hide us completely, even if we had been standing. The tips of the dark grass glowed a very dim orange, sparks erupting from them every few seconds like miniature explosions.

We inched our way farther from the lights of the city and deeper into the grass.

That's when I saw it.

A clearing in the grass. We stopped as we reached the edge of it.

The grass had been burned, from the looks of it, the ground charred and dead. But there in the center was a perfect ring of black roses.

Fear gripped my chest. What did this mean? What had he brought us here to see?

It was much too quiet for me to speak without being heard, so I kept my mouth closed despite my fears. As a group, we hid in the shadows, watching.

After a while, a dark figure, cloaked in rags, floated into the clearing and hovered near the circle of roses. I held back a scream as she turned her head just enough for me to make out her hideous, decaying face.

This was not a demon. I had no idea what this creature was, but she was unnatural. Dark.

Evil.

I covered my mouth and looked away, but in the next instant, my eyes were drawn again to the sight of the creature as she began to cast a spell.

Her arms moved around in a circular motion and a low growling sound hummed in her chest. She threw her head back and laughed as a large cloud of grey and black smoke rose up from the center of the roses. She stepped inside and waited.

From somewhere inside the smoke, voices began to chant. The sound chilled me to my core and I flinched, pulling back. Being here felt wrong. Dangerous.

I wanted to leave and go back to the safety of the castle walls and a life of ignorance.

But at the same time, I knew I was exactly where I was meant to be. This is where my destiny had been leading me ever since the day my brother disappeared. Andros was right. Life would never be the same after tonight.

"Maleia, faithful servant of the Order of Shadows, we invite thee. Wise one, Seeress, Join us now."

A single voice echoed across the clearing and my heart stopped. I watched in horror, knowing that something like this had happened to my brother. Someone from beyond this world had commanded one of these abominations to steal Aerden from me.

Rage boiled inside of me, alongside my fear.

"Prima." The hunter bowed toward the cloud of smoke and for a moment, I caught sight of a shadowed figure on the other side.

I nearly jumped back, unable to control my shock. The girl beside me grabbed my arm, her eyes flashing with fear. She shook her head and I forced stillness upon myself.

"I am your humble servant, now and forever," the creature said.

"Maleia, give us the name of the demon you have chosen for us."

My stomach turned. A name. Another victim like my brother.

"Shyla."

The name rolled off the tongue of the hunter like honey, as if the taste of it was sweet.

"Thank you," the woman in the shadows said. "Your service to this coven is done for now. Set the summoning stone in the roses and depart from us until you are called again."

The huntress bowed low, then floated off into the night. I could no longer see her, but I sensed she had not gone far.

Inside the circle, the voices began chanting again. I couldn't understand what they were saying, but I knew now what Andros had brought us here to see.

He had brought us to a portal like the one I saw in my vision the day Aerden was taken. He was showing us proof that what he'd said was true. A group from the other side—another world—was pulling demons through against their will.

He'd said they didn't know why, but the energy of this ritual was not one of beauty and light. No, these beings served a very dark purpose.

And now they had a name for their next victim.

Shyla.

I glanced toward the village, looking for any sign of a demon girl being brought toward us in shackles like the ones Aerden wore, but the town was completely quiet. Most likely everyone was asleep in their homes.

My attention snapped back to the portal as a bright green light pooled like water inside the circle of roses. The chanting of the voices grew louder and with each repetition, the emerald pool grew larger and brighter.

A terrified scream rang out across the darkness. A girl, but not a demon. No, this voice was different. More fragile somehow. It was coming from someone deep inside the light. Someone on the other side of the portal.

I didn't understand it and even though I strained my eyes toward the light, I couldn't make out what was going on deep inside. I could only see the dark figure I'd seen before. She was wearing a hooded green cloak. A cloak identical to the one the shadowed figure had worn in my vision just before Aerden was ripped from my life.

My stomach twisted.

After more screams, the cloaked figure raised her hands and spoke again. The screams were silenced.

"Shyla, demon of the Shadow World, we call to you. Enter into this sacred place. We demand your presence."

The chorus of voices began a new chant and this time, the emerald light rose up from the ground like an orb.

No. Like a doorway.

Inside the light, a girl lay suspended in mid-air, her body trembling and naked. She was not grotesque and rotting like the creature who had stood here before. She was beautiful and young and terrified.

I gasped. I recognized this race. She was human.

I had heard stories of humans and seen drawings of them in history books, but those same books taught us that the humans were lost to us centuries ago when portal magic was banned by the king. Lea's grandfather.

Something told me this group of humans did not care about the rules of our kingdom. They served a much darker purpose. One that was only then becoming clearer to me.

The chorus of voices continued to chant, but then, a low humming began. More voices? Or was it the sound of the light itself? The green portal grew stronger and brighter.

The light nearly blinded me, blocking out what little view I had of the room beyond.

The group around me tensed and I saw Andros reach for his sword.

This was it. I could feel it in the energy of the air. My muscles froze and tensed as tight as ropes.

Another scream pierced through the darkness, but this time the sound wasn't human.

AN EMERALD LIGHT

THE DEMON'S SCREAM was short-lived. Some invisible force silenced her, but her mouth remained open and contorted. Her dark form was drawn to the summoning stone with the terrifying force of a type of magic I didn't quite understand.

This demon, Shyla, must have been dragged from the false safety of her own bed. Somehow, the ritual had summoned her here in an instant when her name was spoken.

In the bright emerald light her form was a pure black wisp of smoke.

I watched the others in my group, expecting them to stand and fight. But they didn't move. They simply watched. And waited.

Anger rushed through me like a flame. Surely we weren't just going to sit here and do nothing. We could save her. Why weren't they even trying?

I shook my head, trying to make sense of this. A demon was being stolen from our world to who-knows-what kind of torture on the other side. How could we just sit here and watch it happen?

I moved to stand, but the younger demon next to me grabbed my arm again. She shook her head and threw a glance at the green portal.

"Don't," she whispered. "Not yet."

Andros looked back at me, then held up his palm, telling me to be patient.

"I can't just sit here," I said in a harsh whisper. "I'm going to help her."

Andros turned and put his hands on my shoulders, holding me down with a greater strength than I'd known he possessed.

"This is not the time," he said sharply.

"From the looks of it, this is the only time," I said. "They're taking her."

"I know," Andros said. "And keep your voice down. If they discover you, that hunter will be back in an instant and you can kiss us all goodbye. Do you want to die today?"

Hunter. Is that what they called the creature in rags?

I flinched. Every single thread of my being protested against this, but I had to trust him. I knew nothing of the power of this group of humans or their hunter. Well, nothing except the fact that they had been powerful enough to defeat my brother.

The humming inside the portal stopped and I looked over, feeling more helpless than I ever had in my life as the demon's form was sucked through the portal to a foreign world.

I strained to see beyond the light, but I couldn't make out anything at all. Maybe the form of the girl hovering in the light? The green cloak of the leader?

We were losing any chance we might have had. "We have to help her," I said.

"She's beyond our help now," Andros said. "Just watch. I know it's difficult, but you wanted to know the truth. I'm showing you."

I made one last attempt to stand and run after her, believing that if I could get to that green light, maybe I could do something to help.

But Andros held me to the spot, forcing me down toward the ground.

Then, a clear voice rang out from the other dimension.

"Shyla, demon of the Shadow World, we bind you."

The demon's shadow began to seep through the portal to the other side.

I couldn't just sit here and watch this happen. I gathered my strength and tore out of Andros's grasp, rushing from the cover of the tall firegrass and into the clearing.

Inside the light, the hooded woman turned, her eyes meeting mine just as the green portal collapsed downward toward the stone.

"No," I shouted, rushing forward.

The moment I reached the circle of black roses, a strange energy pulled me forward. I lost control of my own form, the force of this dark magic drawing me into its circle.

I cried out, fear freezing me as I felt myself being dragged inside the circle.

The right side of my body crossed into the circle and a great fire sizzled against my flesh, tearing into me like a hot knife. I screamed as several sets of hands grabbed hold of me and pulled me backward.

I fell back against the burned grass, my vision blurring from the pain.

"How stupid can you be?" one of the others yelled. "Andros told you not to intervene."

I couldn't speak. My world was upside down and all I could think of was the intense pain that spread from my foot to my shoulder. Lea appeared at my side, gripping my hand tightly in her own.

"You could have gotten us all killed," the other demon said. She had white eyes the color of snow.

"We have to get out of here," Andros said. "The hunter might be on her way back. The prima, did she see your face?"

I shook my head, not understanding. "I don't know," I said. "Who is the prima?"

"The woman inside the portal. The one with the hooded cloak who was running the ritual. Did she see your face when you stood up?"

I sucked in a breath, my side on fire. I nodded. "She looked right at me."

He cursed. "We have to go. Now."

He placed his hand on my shoulder, then shifted, pulling me with him. The world turned and spun in circles as we flew through the air. I had never moved at such speeds. He led us back through the dark forest, over a pathway that looked as though it were made of pure silver, and finally high into the hills near the northern icelands.

He stopped at the edge of a modest grouping of small huts built out of mud and thick grasses. The remnants of a fire in the center of the space let off a smoldering haze of smoke.

"Where are we?" I asked.

He didn't say anything. He just motioned toward the young demon I'd been next to during the ritual. She laid down a makeshift bed of nettleweeds and willowgrass. Andros set me down on the bed of weeds and I winced at the pain.

"You should have stayed back like I told you," Andros said. He paced the area at my feet. "Don't you think we all wanted to help? Don't you think we would have helped her if we could have?"

I sat up, ignoring the pain as best I could. "I honestly don't know," I said. "We were feet away from one of our own kind being stolen from us and we did nothing. Six powerful demons against what? A group of humans?"

Andros's lips curled up into a grimace of disbelief. "You really are stupid, aren't you? Do you think a normal group of humans can just conjure a portal and summon a demon into their world?"

I couldn't answer. I knew almost nothing of the humans other than what I'd read in storybooks, as a child.

"Humans don't have magic," Lea said. "At least that's what I had always believed."

"No, normal humans don't have magical powers like we do, but centuries ago, when portal magic was first discovered, demons traveled from our world to theirs. Some of those demons even mated with humans," he explained. "When a child is born from both a demon and a human, they are often born with magical powers. Even humans born several generations later will have these powers. Every single human witch is a descendant of a demon. Their magic is supposed to be much weaker than our own, diluted by blood. But somehow these witches—this Order of Shadows—are growing stronger than even we can understand."

"The Order of Shadows," I said, repeating him. "Is that what they are called?"

"Yes," the white-eyed demon woman said. "They are a coven of witches with evil intentions. They have been taking demons from our world for years now."

"What will they do to her?" I asked, my voice trembling. I thought of my brother. "What will they do to the demon girl who was taken?"

Andros ran a hand across his face. "We don't know," he said. "We can only ever catch glimpses of shadows and figures through the light."

"The emerald light," I said. Something triggered my memory and it hit me so hard I had to lie back for a moment.

"What is it?" Lea asked, leaning over me, her face etched with worry.

I closed my eyes, thinking back to the day Aerden was taken. The day of our engagement ceremony. After I passed out, I was taken into the king's chambers where they asked me to tell them what I'd seen in my vision.

When I mentioned that I'd seen a portal—a bright light inside the black roses—my mother had asked me if it was an emerald light.

Hot tears welled up in my eyes. "Andros was telling us the truth," I said to Lea. I opened my eyes as a tear escaped down the side of my face. I struggled to sit up, then took her hand in mine. "Our parents do know what's happening here. This is the proof, Lea, don't you see?"

She shook her head. "I agree this is a horrible thing, but there's no proof here that our parents know this is happening. I won't believe it."

"My mother knew," I said. "When Aerden was taken, it was a blue light I saw, not a green one like tonight. But my mother, don't you remember? She specifically asked me if I had seen an emerald light."

Lea looked away, toward the fresh fire that had been built in the center of the small village. Tears gleamed in her eyes, and I knew she remembered it too.

"It was them," Lea said. "That's what your mother said when you'd finished telling your story."

I nodded, the burn of this betrayal more painful that the real physical burn down my side.

"They've known about the Order all along, haven't they?" she asked, looking up at Andros.

"Yes," he said. "I'm sorry to be the one to bring you this pain, but it was a truth you needed to know."

"The king has gone to great lengths to suppress the truth of what's happening in the villages," the white-eyed demon said. "He has sent guards out to the houses of those who have lost loved ones, demanding their silence in loyalty to the crown."

Lea closed her eyes. She looked tired and suddenly older than I remembered, as if she had aged a decade in the blink of an eye.

"What is your name?" I asked the demon with the white eyes and matching white hair.

"Ourelia," she said with a slight bow of her head. "I am sorry we had to meet on such terms."

"Me, too," I said. I looked to the younger demon who had been by my side during the ritual.

She bowed her head. "My name is Azira," she said. She nodded to a larger demon who was busy putting food out on a roughly made wooden table nearby. "And he is Washan."

"Our group is small but we are growing in numbers," Andros said. "All told, The Resistance boasts about seventy members. Some of us have set up our homes here in this camp near the border of the icelands, while others still choose to live in their own villages for now. Someday we hope to build a city for ourselves where we can train our armies properly."

"The king would never allow it," Lea said.

"Perhaps not," Andros said, one eyebrow raised. "But the king does not know everything."

Lea narrowed her eyes at him. "What do you do—this army of yours?"

"We pay attention," Andros said. "We seek the truth."

"But you do not fight," I said. "Why?"

"We used to," Ourelia said, sadness creeping in to her tone. "But the Order is too strong. We have lost many friends to them over the years."

"Our goal now is to watch and learn," Andros said. "We gain power through knowledge. The more we know about the Order of Shadows, the more powerful we become."

"And what did you learn tonight?" Lea asked.

"Every time a portal opens, we see the same things. We hear the same ritual being repeated, but we can't figure out exactly what they're doing with the demons they take. And there is always a human girl as well, hovering in the light. She is always young and always afraid."

"A sacrifice of some kind?" Lea asked.

"That would explain her fear," Ourelia said. "Death can be a powerful thing."

"In our world, when one of our elders passes on, it's a choice," Azira said softly. "A loving choice that gives us great power. When the energy left behind is poured into a soul stone, it's strong enough to power an entire city for decades. Centuries even, if the demon's spirit was strong. That act of self-sacrifice is powerful enough to allow a new life to be born into this world. Maybe it's similar in the human world in that a sacrifice is a way to gain power."

"If that human girl died tonight, it was definitely not her own choice," I said. "She was terrified."

"No, but maybe their ritual is a way of exchanging one life for a greater, more powerful one," Andros said. "Maybe it is through sacrificing a human life that they are able to summon a demon to take her place?"

We all thought about it for a moment and the forest grew quiet except for the sound of the nightbirds overhead.

The fact was that Andros and his friends had no idea what was really going on in that ritual. They were guessing about most of it.

"How many of these rituals have you witnessed?" I asked.

"I have seen five," Ourelia said. "The most of anyone."

She moved to sit on a stump near the fire.

"I was just a child the first time," she said. "A shadowling of only seven years. I should have been at home in my bed, but on that night there was a starshower unlike any in ages. I left my warm bed and came out to the field to watch the stars. I lay down in the firegrass and stared up at the sky. It was the most beautiful thing I'd ever seen in my young life."

She hung her head low so I could no longer see her eyes.

"I accidentally fell asleep in the grass, but I heard the scream and woke up, scared to death. It was my mother's voice. A single, terrified scream that rang out and then was cut short, like her throat had been sliced with a dagger. I couldn't move. I was completely helpless as I watched her writhing there above the summoning stone, a pool of emerald green light growing against the darkness of the night. I heard the human witch call her name. And then she was gone."

Ourelia sobbed and Andros joined her on the stump, wrapping his arms around her small frame.

"I ran to her, just as you did tonight," she continued. "I tried to figure out where she had gone and what I could do to save her. But the light was gone and I was frightened. I saw the silhouette of the black roses on the ground, but I could feel the strange pull and power of them. I knew they were enchanted somehow, but at the time, I didn't understand the magic. The very idea of such a dark magic was so foreign to me, I thought maybe I'd been dreaming.

"And then I heard the hunter approaching. She slithered out of the darkness like a snake, floating just above the ground. I think the hunters are somehow tied to their portals," she said. "And whenever someone comes near them, they appear in order to protect them. I thought she had come to kill me, and maybe she had, but she laughed when she saw that I was so young. Weak she called me. I wept and she laughed. She told me my mother was lost forever. That she had been taken to a place where her powers would be appreciated."

I sucked in a breath. "That's what Aerden told me," I said.

"Your brother?" Andros asked, surprised. "When?"

"The day before he disappeared. We had an argument and he told me he was leaving the city," I said. I looked to Lea, then looked down at my hands. She didn't know everything I'd talked to Aerden about that day, so I chose my words carefully. "He said he'd met a woman who had told him of a great land where his powers would be appreciated and used. But he'd said she was beautiful. Not a hunter."

Andros shook his head. "That doesn't make sense," he said. "Usually a demon doesn't know they are going to be taken. It doesn't fit somehow. What else do you remember? What did you see when you had your vision of him being taken?"

"The portal light was blue, not green," I said. "And he was shackled with spiked cuffs on his wrists and legs."

"Strange," Andros said, standing and stroking his face.

"It's late and we've talked enough for one night," Ourelia said, touching his arm gently. "Let's eat and rest. We'll have plenty of time to work through the details later."

The demons in the camp all moved to gather around the table. Lea helped me stand and I took a seat next to Ourelia.

"I'm sorry," I said. "About your mother."

"I know it is difficult to watch and do nothing. Believe me when I say there is no one here who thirsts for vengeance more than I do," she said. "If I could, I would kill every hunter in this world and every witch in the next. But we have to be smart. Until we understand them better, their power is too much for us."

"Someday, we will have our vengeance," Andros said, taking Ourelia's hand in his.

After that, talk around the table turned to introductions and food and questions about living in the castle, but I focused all my thoughts on that one word left ringing in my ears.

Vengeance.

HEALER

I AWOKE TO PAIN. I hissed in and sat up. Azira knelt beside my bed on the floor, applying some kind of paste to my wounds.

"I'm sorry I woke you," she said in a whisper. "My father was a shaman and he taught me how to make a few poultices with herbs common to this area. It took me a few hours to find everything I needed, but I am hoping this will help you."

I saw she had cut a long slit along the leg of my pants where the roses had burned me. The healing paste had a foul, swampy odor, but the areas where it was sinking in felt cool.

"Thank you," I said. "It's helping already."

I glanced around the campsite. After dinner, most of the demons had retreated to their own huts. Lea and I had discussed heading home for the night, but Andros had insisted we stay. With my leg still hurting, I agreed. I wasn't sure I was ready to face my parents right now, anyway. Azira and Ourelia had set up soft beds of blankets and rags near the fire for us. Lea was sleeping soundly on the opposite side of the fire, her face so peaceful in the flickering light.

"The herbs will draw the heat away from the burns," Azira said.

I lifted my shirt over my head and nodded toward the ointment. "May I?"

"Of course," she said, sliding it toward me before going back to work on my leg.

I dipped my hand into the paste and rubbed it along my side. As soon as my hand touched the burns on my chest, an unexpected energy flowed through me. I pulled away, surprised. The area I had touched tingled, then cooled.

"What is it?" she asked.

"I don't know," I said, shaking my head. "I just had the strangest surge of energy."

Her eyes grew wide with wonder.

She grabbed my shirt from the ground and wiped the healing ointment from my side. "You're a healer," she said.

I shook my head to protest, but when I looked down, I saw that the wounded area was nearly healed while the untouched spots were still red and blistered.

"It has to be the ointment," I said.

"No. This ointment is very basic," she said. "It takes days to heal burns this deep. Look."

She used my shirt to wipe a small section of the paste off my leg. Underneath, the burns were still red and puffy.

"How is this possible?" I asked. "I would have known if I had a gift like this."

"Not necessarily," she said. "For one, many of our gifts do not present themselves until we are older. Everyone knows that. And second, you probably haven't had many injuries in your lifetime, seeing as how you grew up in the king's city under the protection of the crown."

I stared down at my side, twisting to get a better view. This was incredible.

I dipped my hand into the paste and rubbed it along the small section of my leg she had treated earlier. Again, the strange energy pulsed through me, cooling the burns as if I had placed ice against my skin.

Azira waited a moment, then removed the paste. The skin underneath was still a little red, but nothing like it had been a moment ago.

She laughed, then covered her mouth as Lea muttered and rolled over.

"You have two gifts," she said. "Night vision and healing. Although, I would guess neither of these are your primary gift. What else can you do?"

She pushed the ointment toward me again and I worked, placing the paste all along my right side where the magic of the roses had burned me.

"I can manipulate water," I said. "I'm especially good with ice. My brother Aerden was my opposite, controlling fire."

Sadness seeped into my voice. Ice and fire were not rare gifts, but as a team, we were a perfect pair.

"You miss him greatly," she said. "I have never met twins before."

"I feel like a part of me has been severed."

"I understand," she said, lowering her eyes to the ground.

And I think she did. I could hear it in her voice and see it in her face. Who had she lost? I had been so wrapped up in my own sadness these past ten years I had failed to see the sadness of so many around me.

She didn't ask about my other gifts, but I knew I still had one more. It still hadn't matured to its full power, I didn't think, but it was much rarer and possibly much more valuable.

I could see visions of the future.

And all these visions had told me so far was that things were going to get a lot worse before they would ever get better.

WE WILL SAVE EVERYONE

*W*HEN MORNING CAME, my wounds were almost completely healed.

"Incredible," Andros said, staring at my leg. "This is a very useful gift, my friend. We could really use a healer in our camp."

Lea and I exchanged glances.

We had only briefly talked about what we would do if Andros's information seemed to be true or interesting. Before we saw the portal ritual, Lea had been convinced going to her father was the right thing to do. I hoped she wasn't still thinking of talking to him about what we'd seen. Especially now that we could be sure our parents already had some awareness of what's been going on.

Still, I couldn't promise anything to Andros without speaking with her. Even if our future was uncertain, she was still, technically, my promised mate and I owed her that respect.

Andros nodded. "I understand that you will want to discuss this," he said. "But I'm going to ask you to please not speak with the king about The Resistance. It would put all of us in danger."

Lea hesitated, but then held her hand out toward Andros. "I give you my word that for now I will not discuss the specifics of what we've seen with my father. I promise not to tell anyone of your camp here on the border of the icelands."

Andros took her hand and bowed his head to her. "Thank you, Princess."

"What are your intentions with this Resistance Army?" I asked. "What do you hope to accomplish?"

Andros stepped back and clasped his hands behind him. "We want to destroy the Order of Shadows," he said simply, as if it were an achievable task.

"And how do you plan to go about doing that?" Lea asked. She looked around the small group gathered in the camp. They were hardly an army.

"First, we will gather as much information about them as we can. Once we know how they work, what magic they are using and what weaknesses they may have, we will start to develop a plan of attack," he said. "We will continue to recruit those who would join us and fight with us. And, eventually, we will start a war against these humans. We will not stop until they are dead and the portals are destroyed."

"And what about the demons on the other side?" I asked, thinking of Aerden. "Do you hope to develop a plan for rescuing them?"

"If they can be rescued," Andros said. "We don't have enough information about what's going on once the demons are pulled through to know if they can be saved."

"But if they can be saved—"

"Then we will save everyone," Andros said. "And I hope you'll be there by my side. As future rulers of the kingdom, your commitment to The Resistance would mean more than you can know."

Lea nodded, then raised an eyebrow toward me.

I bowed to Andros. "Thank you for your hospitality last night," I said. "And for trusting us with what you have learned so far. We have a lot to discuss."

Andros stepped toward me. "I'm truly sorry for the loss of your brother, but if you join us, I promise I will do everything in my power to help you either save him or avenge his memory," he said. "You have my word."

I placed my hand on his shoulder. "Thank you, my friend."

Lea and I gathered our weapons and started toward the road.

Andros called out, stopping us at the edge of the village. "Be careful on the way home," he said. "The witch last night saw your face."

"What does that mean?" I asked.

"It means she'll be looking for you," he said.

A chill ran up my spine. Looking for me?

"And what do I do if she finds me?" I asked him.

He raised an eyebrow and the left side of his mouth curled into a smile. "Run."

THIS WOUND CARRIED POISON

*I*T WAS A long trip home. Once we got closer to the castle, we decided to walk instead of fly, hoping that by not using any magic, the guards at the gate would not be able to track our path back to the camp.

At this point, I wouldn't have been surprised if the king had instructed some of his personal sentinels to follow us.

I wanted to discuss our plans, but I was scared to hear what Lea would have to say. I knew she wouldn't want to openly betray her father by joining The Resistance. And how could I join without openly betraying her in the process?

But I wanted to join them.

I wanted to see the end of the Order of Shadows.

"Just say it." After miles of walking in silence, Lea finally stopped and turned to me. "I know what you're thinking. I can feel the anger and worry coming off you. Let's just get it out in the open."

I took a deep breath. How could I convince her to want what I wanted?

"I want to join them," I said. "They're my best hope of finding my brother."

"They are a disorganized group of rebels," Lea said. "They may call themselves an army, but other than Andros, there's not a warrior among them, that I saw. What hope do they ever have of defeating those witches?"

"More than I have of defeating them on my own," I said.

Lea pressed her lips together, fuming. "You would risk everything we have to go after a group of human witches you know nothing about? You would risk your life? Our future?" Her voice softened. "Our love?"

I closed my eyes and turned to look at the king's city rising up in the distance, still several miles away. "What would you have me do, Lea? Are you going to tell me to just forget him? To let him go and to move on? You know I can't do that," I said. "Especially after what we've seen. This group, the Order of Shadows, is taking demons all the time. Fathers, brothers, sisters. Gone in the blink of an eye. As the leader of our people, would you be able to turn your back on this?"

"I'm not the leader yet," she said. "And neither are you. It's my father's job to make those kinds of decisions. He's very wise and very careful. For whatever reason, he's decided not to fight. Maybe he knows just how dangerous they really are. Maybe he knows something Andros doesn't know. Until we've spoken with him, we won't know the true reasons for his actions."

"So you still want to tell him?"

She shrugged. "I don't know," she said. "If he's gone to such great lengths to hide this from us, then he may not even listen to what we have to say. Or he may get angry that we went looking for answers on our own."

"Do you think we'd have any hope of changing his mind?" I asked. I shook my head. "If he already knows the truth, he's not going to suddenly stand and fight. He's done nothing to help us find answers about Aerden, and I don't think telling him what we know is going to change that."

"Maybe not," she said. "But I feel like I need to at least give him a chance to tell his side of the story."

I took another deep breath. It was hard to know which path to take. There was no doubt the king's army would be much more effective against the Order of Shadows, but why had the king refused to fight?

"Let's just let it sit for a while," she said, moving closer to my side. When she put her hand in mine, I tensed. "Maybe after we've put some time and distance between us and what we witnessed last night, we'll have a better picture of what we want to do. I don't want to lose you, but I also don't want to betray my father. We'd lose everything, Denaer. He would never forgive us if we joined a rebel's army."

"I know," I said. I pulled my hand away. "But every day that goes by is another day Aerden may be in danger. What if he is still alive on the other side? What if he's being tortured? What if—"

Something moved at the corner of my vision. A streak of orange and white flying through the air toward me.

I turned and placed myself in front of Lea as a creature pounced on top of me. I cried out as its claws ripped through my side.

"Run," I shouted to Lea, but she didn't run. She raised her bow toward the beast.

I pushed against the soft coat of the orange-striped beast as it bared sharp white teeth in a horrible hiss.

Lea's arrow sliced through the air toward us, but before she hit her target, a second creature jumped out of nowhere, pushing her toward the ground. Lea managed to shift before her body touched the ground. The beast passed through Lea's smoke, then skidded against the dirt and grass, disoriented.

I managed to push the first beast off of me, but the pain in my side kept me from being able to focus enough to shift into smoke. I reached for the axe I now carried with me everywhere. Aerden's axe. It had been his favorite weapon and wearing it had helped me to feel closer to him. I was grateful I had it with me now.

Lea and I moved toward each other, pressing our backs together, weapons ready.

The two orange beasts looked almost identical except that one was adorned with black stripes while the other had white stripes that ran the length of its body. I'd never seen anything like them before in all my travels.

"What are these things?" I asked.

"I'm not sure," Lea answered. "I've never seen them before."

We moved together as the beasts circled around us, their teeth dripping with saliva as they growled at us.

There was only one explanation as to who had sent these beasts after us. The cloaked witch who had seen my face during the ritual last night. She must have sent them to find me.

Blood flowed from the wound in my side. That was the second time in two days that I had been injured, but I already knew that this was much worse than the burns I sustained during last night's ritual. This wound carried poison through my body. I felt it seeping into me, weakening my magic, and flushing me with fever.

I stumbled and clutched at my side, feeling weak.

"Are you okay?" Lea asked, her voice panicked.

"I don't know," I said. "I think it poisoned me."

I coughed and fell to my knees, barely able to hold the axe up any longer.

Lea kept her bow raised, pointing it between the two beasts as they circled.

Anger tightened my chest. Andros had warned me that I was in danger and yet we had stopped in the middle of a field to argue. How could we have been so careless? How could I be so weak and useless?

If I made it through this, I would dedicate myself to training. I would become a warrior so great no beast could overcome me this easily.

If I made it through.

I placed my hand against the bleeding wound, then closed my eyes. I took several deep breaths, trying to reconnect with the healing power I had discovered last night. It took several tries, but eventually, the familiar tingle of the cool healing power flowed from my hand. It wasn't enough to completely stop whatever poison was already in my system, but it was enough to dull the pain and allow me to gather my strength.

I stood and the two beasts came together, surprise in their black eyes.

I tensed, prepared for them to strike. Only they didn't. Instead, they did the one thing I never could have expected.

They shifted.

NO ONE COMPARED TO OUR MISTRESS

THE BODIES OF the beasts straightened inside a cloud of dark smoke.

I watched in shock. There were similarities of a demon's shifting, but it was incredibly different at the same time. There was a swirl of smoke and shadow, but their bodies never completely disappeared. It happened so quickly, I couldn't make complete sense of it.

Were they part demon?

But when their new forms appeared, I had my answer.

They were human. Witches from the Order of Shadows. I was sure of it.

And they were twins.

I choked down a lump in my throat. What cruelty was this? Sending human twins here to destroy me as punishment for what I had seen? Whoever had sent them must have recognized me somehow. They must have known my connection to Aerden.

The realization of it gave me new strength. New rage.

I narrowed my eyes. "Who are you?" I demanded. "Did the emerald prima send you?"

"The emerald prima?" The girl on the left had long hair that was so blond, it was almost white. Her face and form were completely identical to the girl on her right. The only difference between them was the color of their hair. "The prima who saw you at the ritual last night is no one compared to our mistress."

The auburn-haired girl at her side smiled. "We have a message for you," she said. "For both of you."

"Priestess Winter says to stop looking for your brother," the white-haired witch said. "He belongs to the Order of Shadows now and there is nothing you can do. He is bound to another with an unbreakable magic. Let him go or you will suffer the same fate."

"What magic?" I asked. "Who is Priestess Winter?"

"It's better if you learn to stop asking questions," she said. "Out of respect for the position of both your families, your life will be spared today, but if we have to come looking for you again, it will not end quite so favorably."

I glared at the two witches. "How dare you come here to threaten me," I said, standing up as straight as the pain would allow. "Aerden was more than just a brother to me. He was my twin. As twins, you should understand what that means. I won't stop searching for him, and if you come after me again, it will be you who suffers an unfavorable end."

The girl with white hair smiled and laughed, then took a few steps toward me. She lifted her hand and a bright white light formed on the tips of her fingers. With an effortless wave of her hand, our weapons fell to the ground, clanging against each other in the grass.

"Your words are strong and I have no doubt your love for your brother is even stronger," she said, moving close enough to me that I could feel her warmth. "But you have no idea the power you are up against, demon. Let this go."

With that, the twins shifted back to their beastly forms, running into the distance as quickly as they had come.

EIGHTEEN
THE HUMAN WORLD, PRESENT DAY

I RAN MY HAND along the jagged red scar that still marred the side of my body. It was the only wound I had that was deep enough to scar my body permanently. No matter which form I took, that scar always remained.

Remembering just how weak and helpless I had been back then was difficult. It helped some, knowing that I had eventually seen the end of those tiger twins, but their deaths had not come at my hands. It had been Harper who had ended them.

She was stronger than all of us.

I had a feeling she had only just barely begun to realize the depth of her own power. Half-demon. Half-human. The daughter of a king and a prima. She was one of a kind, but because of that, the hope of both our worlds rested on her shoulders. It was a lot for a seventeen-year-old to handle.

I turned and smiled as Harper walked out the back door and made her way toward me in the garden.

No, not seventeen. She was eighteen.

Today was her eighteenth birthday. The day she should have become the prima here in the town of Peachville. It was a day I had dreaded since the moment her lips first touched mine.

I never dreamed we would be able to destroy the Peachville demon gate and free both her and my brother from the Order of Shadows. It was a miracle we were thankful for every single day. But especially this day.

"What are you thinking about?" she asked, laughing. "You look happier than you have all night."

"I was just thinking how wonderful it is that there's no binding ritual tonight," I said, pulling her into my arms under the light of the moon. "How grateful I am that you will never be prima."

She wrapped her arms around me and laid her head against my chest. "There are still so many gates," she said. "So many girls and demons being forced into a life of slavery to the Order of Shadows. It's hard to be truly happy when there's still so much that needs to be done. There are still so many who need to be saved."

I kissed the top of her head. "And we will save them all," I said. "One battle at a time."

I didn't want to tell her that our next battle was just around the corner.

I wanted to let her enjoy this one night without worry. I had kept the drawings of my most recent vision secret from her, but I couldn't hold it back forever.

That's why I needed to give her this memory stone tonight. I wanted to face the future knowing there was nothing left unsaid between us. I wanted to be able to stand before her with no secrets and no doubts.

She pulled away and lifted up on her toes to place a soft kiss on my cheek. "I know you're busy with some secret project, and I didn't mean to interrupt you, but I just wanted to make sure you were okay out here all by yourself."

I placed my hands on her cheeks. "I love you, Harper."

Her eyes searched mine. "I love you, too," she whispered.

I lowered my lips to hers, drawing courage from the feel of her body pressed against mine. I would need courage to face the memories that came next.

NEVER HAVE TO ASK
THE SHADOW WORLD, 75 YEARS AGO

THE TIGER'S WOUND had carried enough poison to bring me to the edge of death, but not enough to finish the job.

Lea had managed to help me back to the castle, but I had collapsed against the steps, unable to go any farther. My body had been consumed by a terrible fever and my mind was lost to reality.

For days I lay trapped in a nightmare, visions of burning bodies and tortured demons pulling me deeper into madness.

When I finally regained consciousness several days later, I was weak and broken.

I had been so foolish to believe I could fight the Order of Shadows on my own. In my rage, I had imagined myself strong and capable, but the truth was that I had no training and no knowledge about how to fight against human witches. I didn't know the first thing about their magic or their power.

Aerden had been one of the strongest, most capable fighters I'd ever known, yet I had watched as he was shackled and torn from this world; fear and pain contorting his features.

In one brief moment, a witch with the power to somehow transform herself into a terrible beast had struck me down. She could have killed me if she'd wanted.

When I first woke up, part of me had almost wished she had finished the job.

I would rather have died than face the extent of my own shame and weakness.

I drifted in and out of consciousness for several days. Often, Lea would be there by my side, reading to me or holding my hand. Sometimes I woke to see my mother's worried face.

But when I opened my eyes and found the king standing beside my bed, I forced myself to sit up.

I struggled to focus on his face and saw right away that he was angry. I knew he had come here with a specific purpose. And it wasn't a happy one.

"Denaer, I know you need your rest, but I am glad to see you awake," he said. He pulled a chair over to my bedside and sat down so that his face was level with my own. "There is something very important I need to talk about with you, and I need to make sure that you hear every single word. Do you understand?"

"Yes, your majesty," I said. My voice was scratchy and weak and I reached for a cup of water on the table. My hands were still so weak that even the simple act of picking up a glass was difficult and awkward. At the time, I had no grasp of how long I had been unconscious or just how close to death I had truly come.

"Lea has been very vague about the wound on your side and how you came to be so sick, but I know the poison that runs through your system," he said. "I know that you are very lucky to be alive."

I dared not say a word. If he knew this poison, then he also knew that I had discovered the truth about the Order of Shadows. Or at least some part of the truth.

"I understand that losing your brother was the cause of great sorrow in your life. I even understand your need to continue searching for answers when your parents repeatedly asked you to leave it alone," he said. "What I don't understand is why you insist on dragging my daughter, the future Queen of the North, into dangerous situations with no regard for her safety."

I turned to stare at him, meeting his gaze. This was not about putting his daughter in danger and we both knew it.

"Lea makes her own choices," I said.

"She would follow you to the edge of this world and beyond if you asked her and don't pretend she wouldn't," he said. "Your searching has gone far enough. You've already come dangerously close to a truth I hoped you would never have to face. You cannot go any farther down that path. It's time for you to accept that your brother is gone and he's never coming back. It's time for you to embrace your future here with the princess and let go of the past."

My hands trembled in anger and I balled them into tight fists. How dare he ask me to turn my back on my own brother? He should have been offering his help, his guards, his money, and influence. He should have been apologizing for letting things go as far as they had.

"You're right," I said, sitting up a little straighter. My anger was giving me a renewed sense of strength.

He nodded. "I'm glad to hear you have finally come around to this under—"

"You're right that we have discovered a terrible truth," I said, interrupting him. "We know all about the Order of Shadows. We know that these human witches have portals all over the Northern Kingdom. They steal demons from their homes in the middle of the night and pull them through to their world for their own evil purpose. And we know that you've known about this since before my brother was taken, yet you did nothing to stop them."

"You don't know anything," the king said, standing. "Don't speak to me as if you have the right to judge my actions. I am King of the North and I will make the decisions I feel are best for my people."

"Then tell me, King, how is it best for the people that these witches are allowed to continue taking demons from their villages?" I asked. I swung my legs over the side of my bed.

"I don't answer to you." His voice swelled.

"You do answer to me," I said. I set my feet against the floor and somehow found the strength to stand for the first time in days. "My brother is gone because of the decisions you have made and the lies you have told. You owe me an answer. You owe it to every demon who has lost someone they love."

The king's face twisted in anger.

"You have no idea what you are talking about. The Order of Shadows is not a normal enemy," he said. "I cannot simply send out my army and destroy them."

"How would you know unless you tried?" I asked. "Their portals are unguarded. I have seen one of their rituals with my own eyes. There was no one there to stand against them. Not a single guard or sentinel."

The king lifted his chin and squared his shoulders. "The demons who live inside the gates of this city live in safety," he said. "I do the best I can to send out patrols to watch over the villages in the outerlands, but it's impossible to police them all. The Order is too big and too strong. If I sent my guards out there, they would all be dead in an instant. What use is that to anyone?"

"What use is a king who is too scared to fight back?" I asked, taking my first steps. "As long as the Order knows you are afraid of them, they will continue to take until there is nothing left."

"We are immortal," he said. "The humans are not. Their lives are short and meaningless compared to ours. Yes, what the Order of Shadows is doing is horrible. But they control very dark magic that is nearly impossible to defeat. It's in the best interest of the kingdom to wait them out. They cannot live forever."

I could hardly believe what I was hearing. This was his plan? To simply outlive the humans?

Andros was right. The king was blind. Ruled by fear and foolishness.

"And what about the demons who are being taken?" I asked. "You would sacrifice them so willingly?"

"Their sacrifice is minor compared to the lives that would be lost in a war against the humans."

"Maybe, but at least our deaths would be honorable." I walked toward him, fueled by my own anger and determination. "At least we would die standing up against a great evil rather than allowing that evil to rule us through fear. There is no honor in Aerden's death, if he is in fact dead."

The king snapped his head toward me. "He is dead to all of us," he said. "It is best if you learn to accept that now."

"I cannot accept it," I said. "I won't. I will not be ruled by fear."

"You'd rather be ruled by rage?" the king asked. "You're a fool and I won't allow you to drag my daughter any further into your madness."

"That isn't for you to decide." Lea stood in the doorway, tears reflected in her deep green eyes. "I love you, father, but my heart belongs to Denaer. And my life, my future, belongs to the demons of the Northern Kingdom."

The king's face crumbled and he shook his head. "What are you saying?" he asked. "That you would choose to betray me?"

Lea crossed the room and placed her hand in mine. "You betrayed me first. You have betrayed all of us."

I looked down into the face of a girl I had known all my life, but never truly seen as the future queen until that moment. She had more strength than I had ever realized.

"It's not too late to stand and fight," I said. "I know the Order is strong, but every enemy has a weakness. All we have to do is find it."

The king stared down at our joined hands, then turned toward the door. "If you choose to fight, I won't stop you," he said. "But know that the moment you step outside the gates of this city, I will no longer acknowledge you as my daughter. I won't come after you when you are taken by the Order."

He walked through the door of the room, not even turning around to look at his own daughter one last time.

Lea took in a sharp breath but did not let go of her grip on my hand.

We stood together in silence for a moment before she finally turned to me. "Are you strong enough to make it to the camp?" she asked.

I searched her face. "Is this really what you want?" I asked her. "Because if you are doing this for me, I want you to know that I would never ask such a sacrifice from you."

The tears she had been able to hold back in front of her father escaped onto her cheeks. "You should know by now that you would never have to ask," she said.

Her hand slipped from mine.

"Do you want to say goodbye to your parents?" she asked.

I shook my head. "If Aerden is dead to them, then they are dead to me, too."

"Gather anything you want to take with you and then get some rest," she said, wiping the tears from her face. "We'll leave at dawn."

THE LOVE SHE DESERVED

WE ARRIVED AT camp of The Resistance three days later. We'd taken our time getting there since I still hadn't fully recovered from my injuries. Lea was also concerned that her father might have us followed, so she led us on a strange path, taking detours across swamps and into the forest, making it difficult for anyone to track us.

Andros and the others were very happy to see us and they welcomed us into their village and their lives with open arms.

As soon as we were settled, our real training began. Andros took charge of our battle training, sparring with us from early morning until mid-afternoon every day. It was obvious right from the start that we both had a lot to learn.

Everything I thought I knew about fighting was incredibly basic. Beginner stuff that was practically useless in a real battle. But Andros took me under his wing and taught me how to fight like a true warrior. Over time, I improved.

Lea, however, excelled. She was a natural fighter with an affinity for ranged weapons.

At times, I worried that she had followed me here out of loyalty. Or love.

But other times, especially during our training, I saw her anger come through. I recognized her pain.

She had looked up to her father as the perfect example of a ruler and king, but now the veil had been lifted from her eyes. She saw him for the coward he was. And I could see that the truth had changed her. Hardened her. I tried to get her to talk about it, but any time I mentioned her father, she clammed up and refused to speak.

"I'm not his daughter anymore," she would say.

As part of our daily tasks, I took on the job of watering the crops while Lea helped with the cooking. Sometimes after dinner we would walk together, hand-in-hand, and talk about the day's activities.

Sometimes we sat around the fire telling stories of our loved ones and remembering the happier days. Lea curled close to me on the colder nights and I began to like the feel of her warm body pressed against mine.

And I hated myself for it.

Every touch became a betrayal of the worst kind.

It should be Aerden here by her side, not me.

One night, when everyone else had gone to bed, Lea and I stayed up talking by the fire. She ran her fingers lazily across my arm as she began to talk about the future. Our future.

I had no problem talking about the past. Remembering was how I stayed close to Aerden.

But the future she was dreaming about was something I couldn't see. She talked about what we would do after we won the war against the Order of Shadows. How someday we would become the leaders our people truly deserved.

"He cannot deny me the throne," she said of her father. "The people will still accept us as their rightful King and Queen."

She spoke of restoring peace to the land and building a safe home together.

And in time, her talk turned to children.

I stood then, my stomach tight. I walked away from the firelight, my back turned.

She came up behind me, wrapping her arms around my waist, and pressing her face against my back.

"I know it's difficult to imagine a future when we're preparing for battle, but I need this," she said softly. She sounded so vulnerable. "I need to know we still have this hope of a real life together that doesn't involve humans or swords or dark magic. I need to know that the light of your love still shines for me."

I stiffened, unable to return her affection. "And what about Aerden?"

"He'll be right there by our side," she said.

I placed my hand on top of hers, trying to imagine the life she saw so clearly for us. Was there any hope of it?

Even if we could somehow save my brother and bring him back here, I knew he wouldn't be able to live in the city alongside us, watching our happy lives unfold in front of him. That was the whole reason he'd left in the first place.

No, if he ever came back, I swore right then and there that I would tell Lea the truth about the heart stone. I would do what I should have done right from the beginning. I would do whatever it took to make her see that the love she deserved had been right there in front of her all along and that she and Aerden belonged together.

I stepped out of her embrace.

"It's late," I said. "You should get some rest."

Disappointment flooded her eyes. She dropped her hands to her side and looked toward the fire.

"Aren't you coming to bed?" she asked.

I followed her gaze and stared into the flames. She wanted my love for her to burn like that fire, but it never would. It was cruel to draw her in and push her away like this, over and over.

It wasn't fair to her. The future she hoped for did not exist. Not for me.

Eventually she turned away, disappearing into the hut we shared at the edge of the village. My heart ached for her, but it could be no other way.

As time wore on, Lea stopped talking about the future altogether.

ABANDONED

FOR FIFTEEN YEARS we continued on like this.
Our skills in battle became stronger and more refined. Our numbers grew as others learned about our work to restore the villages that had been hit the hardest.

But none of that was enough.

I tried to act patient, but at night after Lea had fallen asleep, I often stayed up and read through the notes Andros had taken about the Order of Shadows. I learned everything I could about them and how their magic worked. I spent a lot of time drawing pictures of the portal rituals; trying to make sense of what was happening. I looked for any kind of clue that might show a weakness or an opportunity to defeat them. I became obsessed.

What was the significance of the circle of black roses? How were the demons summoned to the portal? Were they marked and chosen beforehand? Or did the hunter only need to know their name in order to summon them?

And why was it different when Aerden was taken?

Was he still alive somewhere? Would I ever see him again?

The questions in my head haunted me at night when I let them rule my mind. Some nights I felt like my head would split apart from all the unanswered questions inside. I just wanted to know the truth. I needed answers.

Answers that weren't coming fast enough.

We studied the portals, the stones, the roses. We listened to those who would talk.

But I wanted more.

In my mind, I had started to formulate a plan. If I could just find the portal Aerden was taken through, maybe I could go through long enough to find him and bring him home.

Only, finding the specific blue portal he'd been taken through was harder than it sounded. Some days I felt like I was going to lose my mind if we didn't find it soon.

Then, one day when we were rebuilding some of the houses in Sapuran, we got our first real breakthrough in a decade.

Lea and I were working on the roof of one of the homes when the commotion began. We exchanged worried glances, then got down and rushed to the other side of the village where a group of demons had gathered around Andros and Ourelia.

We pushed through the crowd of worried faces. "What is it?" I asked.

He looked at me with such intensity, my heart nearly stopped. "A new portal has been found," he said.

"What color stones?" I asked, barely able to breathe.

"Blue."

"Show me."

The demon who had found the blue portal took us to a location deep inside the caves of Muro, carved into the side of the Black Cliffs. My heart sank when he brought us to the mouth of the cave.

This couldn't be the place where my brother disappeared. In my vision when he was taken, he had been in an open field, much like the one near Klashok.

Still, finding any portal was a victory.

"How did you find this?" I asked.

The young demon's name was Jericho and he was relatively new to our group. "I grew up near these caves and like to come here sometimes when I want to be alone to think," he said. "So when Andros told us to start looking for signs of portals, I thought maybe this would be a good place to hide one."

"Good job," Andros said. "I had no idea the roses could even grow this deep in the rock."

"The area here looks abandoned," I said. "Is it possible this portal hasn't been used in a long time?"

"Anything is possible," Andros said. He walked around the small circular area here at the end of the cave that housed the portal.

"Do you feel it?" he asked. "Any type of pull toward these roses?"

I moved closer to the circle of black and shook my head. "Not even the slightest bit of magic. And look." I pointed where our footprints had disturbed the dust covering the rocks. "No one has been for a very long time. Years. Maybe decades."

"Why would the Order abandon a portal?" Andros asked.

I knew he didn't expect an answer, but it brought up all kinds of questions in my mind. Had something happened to the witches on the other side? Or maybe the hunter who was supposed to be protecting it? Without the hunter, maybe the portals went inactive?

Frustration ate at my insides. I was so tired of only having these tiny little pieces to the puzzle. We'd been searching for so long. Where were all the answers? What were we missing?

When Andros had said a blue portal had been found, I'd gotten my hopes up, thinking maybe we had found something that would make a difference. Maybe I had finally found Aerden's portal.

But what good was an abandoned portal? An inactive portal was nothing to us. We might never know why the Order abandoned this place.

I paced the area, my anger building with each step. The power inside of me roared to life and I felt like I was on the edge of losing control. I'd been so patient for so long, but at this rate, we might never find the truth about my brother. I couldn't take it anymore. I was so tired of disappointment.

Ice gathered on my fingertips and even though I tried to push it down, it continued to grow until my entire fist was covered with frost.

"Denaer, it's going to be okay," Lea said, touching my shoulder. "We're going to find it."

"When?" I shouted. I pulled away from her, nearly knocking her backward. "When will we find the answers? It's been twenty-five years since Aerden was taken and we're no closer to finding him than we were back then."

In my frustration, I slammed my icy fist against the back wall of the cave, putting more strength into it than I intended to.

The blow thundered through the corridor as my hand punctured the molten rock. Ice spread in a circle around my fist, the rock crackling and splitting as it froze.

I pulled my hand away and backed up, watching as large cracks tore through the icy walls, then shattered like glass.

For a moment, I was afraid the whole place would come down on top of us, burying us inside this cave like a tomb.

But only the back wall tumbled to the ground. A thick spray of fog rose up from the remains of the wall as the warm air in the cave began to melt the ice-encased rock.

I stared ahead, shocked by my own strength.

"Let's get out of here before the whole place caves in," Andros said.

"Wait," I said, just making out the image of something glowing beyond the debris.

I lifted my arm to shield my face and stepped forward, stepping carefully over the rubble.

"What is it?" Lea asked, coming up behind me.

"Do you see it?" I asked. "That blue glow?"

"I do," Jericho, the demon who brought us here, said. "What is it?"

"I don't know." I made my way through the cool misty fog. The wall I'd brought down had been several feet thick, but once I got through the worst of the debris, the corridor opened up into a small room about a quarter of the size of the portal room we'd been standing in.

It was a den of some sort. Rags lay in a pile on the floor at my feet like a nest.

But it wasn't an animal or beast who lived here.

Along the far wall of the space was a bookcase of dusty tomes.

As I stepped forward, something cracked beneath my feet. I looked down and gasped at a scattered collection of human bones.

These rags were not a bed. They were the clothes this creature had been wearing when it died.

"What is it?" Lea asked, finally reaching this side of the fallen wall.

I crouched down. This was exactly the kind of break I'd been waiting for.

I picked up a bone and lifted it into the air.

"It's a dead hunter."

A HIDDEN POWER

*A*NDROS PUSHED FORWARD into the small room. "A dead hunter?" His voice was soft, almost reverent.
He studied the bones and the rags.

"This means they can be killed," he said. "What if the hunter's death is what closed the portal?"

He crossed toward the piles of books and trinkets along the far wall. His hand trembled as he picked up the tattered tome at the top of the stack. He blew a puff of air across the spine and dust flew out from it, hovering in the air for a long moment before fluttering down to join the long-settled decades of dust on the ground.

He crouched low and opened the book, his eyes glued to the pages. His lips parted as he read, his hand slowly rising to his mouth.

"What is it?" Lea asked.

Tension gathered in the room as we waited for him to answer. We'd never found a hunter's den before. We'd never even seen or heard of a dead hunter or known if they were immortal. The true impact of this find hadn't even sunk in yet, but we all understood the importance these books and belongings might have if they contained any kind of information or clues about the Order of Shadows.

The look in Andros's eyes when he turned said it all. Heat spread across my skin and I fell back against the broken wall of the cave.

"I've never seen anything like this before," Andros said. He turned the page and scanned the contents, his breath coming faster. "There are spells in here. I can't understand all of it, but some things are familiar. And there are diagrams. Maps."

"Maps?" I asked, my heart squeezing. "What kind of maps?"

"I'm not sure," he said. "I think they might be maps of the human world."

"What about the other books there?" I asked.

Andros set the first book down and Lea and I joined him near the wall to look through the other items. Ourelia and Jericho searched the rest of the small room.

"Look at this," Lea said. She sat down in the dust and reached out for a faintly-glowing stone half-covered in dirt and grime.

The moment her fingers touched the stone, her eyes went wide and all the breath was pushed from her chest. She looked at me, terror darkening her eyes as they clouded from green to black. She reached for me, clutching my wrist.

In an instant, the ground fell out from underneath us. The world spun in circles and I had to fight to stay upright. I was blinded for a moment, unable to tell where we were or what had happened.

But then, we landed in a new time and place. When my sight returned to me, we were standing in the hallway of a strange building.

I had no idea how we'd gotten there, but something was definitely off about the whole thing.

Two human women stood in front of us talking, but neither of them seemed to have even noticed our presence. The color of this place was off, too, as if we were in a faded version of reality, the edges of every surface slightly blurred and muted.

As if we were caught in a dream.

"What's happening?" I whispered, backing away from the women.

"I have no idea," Lea said. She looked down at the small round stone in her palm. "Somehow this stone brought us here, but I have no idea where here is."

"Why haven't they even turned to look at us?" I asked.

Lea studied the women. Carefully, she stepped forward, walking around them and even between them. She lifted her hand up in front of one of the women's faces, but the woman continued her conversation without so much as blinking.

"They can't see us," she said.

Behind me, Andros suddenly appeared in the hallway. It took him a moment to catch his breath, but when he did, he was actually smiling.

"Do you understand what's happening?" I asked him.

"As if it wasn't enough for us to discover a dead hunter and her spell books today, we've also discovered a hidden power of Lea's."

"I did this?" she asked. She put her hand straight through one of the women's bodies, as if we were merely watching an apparition or a memory.

"I've heard of this ability but never actually known anyone who could do it," he said. "When you touched that stone, it somehow triggered a memory. But not one of your memories. One of the stone's memories."

She shook her head. "A stone can have memories?"

"Yes," he said. "Everything has memories. Demons, places, objects. Something about this stone held a memory so strong it triggered your ability to see this memory. And in fact, not just see the memory, but also to relive it."

"So what we're seeing here is a memory?"

"Yes," he said. "We're inside the stone's memory. Look."

He pointed to the two human women. The taller one, an older woman with white hair, took out a small box and presented it to the younger woman.

"Why can't we hear what they're saying?" I asked.

Andros shook his head. "I'm not sure," he said. "It could be that this is a new power and Lea will need to work to gain more control over it, or it could be that her powers don't manifest sound at all. Only time will tell just how strong an ability this will be for her."

The younger woman opened the box, tears in her eyes. She gasped at the blue stone inside, happiness and gratitude in her expression.

But as the older woman took the stone from the box, something about the memory darkened. My stomach twisted as she grabbed the younger woman's hand and forced the stone against her skin.

The young girl's mouth curled into a painful grimace and her legs gave out from under her. She fell to the ground, but the older woman never let go. Instead, she slowly couched to the floor, keeping the stone pressed firmly against the other woman's palm. She was saying something furiously and as she spoke, the younger woman's skin began to wrinkle and dry, as if sucking the life directly out of her body. Her hair began to fall out in patches and her eyes dulled.

When the spell was complete, the older woman smiled and stood. She straightened the skirts of her gown and tossed the blue stone at the younger woman's broken body.

She wasn't dead, but she was changed. She was turning into a hunter. I don't know how I knew it, but I was sure that was what we had just witnessed.

Then, as suddenly as we'd appeared in that place, we left it again, sucked back through time and space until we stood, once again, firmly on the dusty floor of the forgotten cave.

MEMORY KEEPER

I STUMBLED WHEN WE reappeared inside the cave, falling against the crumbling wall. My stomach lurched and I leaned forward, feeling like I was going to throw up.

"What the hell just happened?" Ourelia asked.

Andros and Lea took a moment to catch their breath and regain their footing before either of them answered her.

"Lea's a memory keeper," he said.

Ourelia's eyes grew wide and her mouth fell open in awe.

"I never knew I could do that," Lea said. "That was insane."

She laughed, but then almost collapsed. I stepped forward and caught her before she hit the ground.

"Are you okay?" I asked.

Her eyes fluttered open and she gave me a weak smile. "I think so," she said. "I think I just need a few minutes to recover. That was amazing."

"It's more than amazing," Andros said. "It's a rare and very important gift. I have heard rumors that your father, the king, also possesses this gift, but I never believed it was true until this moment."

Lea looked up at him with questions in her eyes. "My father has this memory gift? I've never heard anyone speak of it my entire life," she said.

"I honestly thought it was just a rumor, but now that I've seen you with the same gift, I feel certain your father must also possess this same power."

"Why would he keep it hidden?" she asked. She tried to stand, but was still too weak. I let her lean against me.

"I am not sure," he said. "Either he has a good reason to believe the rest of the kingdom does not need to know about this power or..."

His voice trailed off and he turned away.

"Or what?" I asked.

He rubbed his hand across his cheek, thinking. "Rare abilities like this are often passed down to the next generation," he said. "Maybe your father never told you about this because he was afraid you might also have the same ability."

Lea shook her head. "Why would he be afraid of that? Why wouldn't he want to help me discover all of my abilities so that I could be the strongest leader I could be someday?"

Andros paced in front of us. "A memory keeper can be very dangerous to someone who is trying to keep secrets," he said. "Like I told you before, everything has memory. Even places. If you had stumbled upon this ability in the middle of the throne room, for example, just think of what you might have been able to learn. You could have used your ability to uncover all of his secrets."

Lea fell back against my chest.

What Andros was saying made perfect sense. If a young Lazalea had been encouraged to develop this power, she might have wanted to practice throughout the castle. She might have discovered some secret conversations or touched an item that held an important memory he didn't want her to know about.

Considering how far he'd gone to keep the Order of Shadows a secret, I didn't doubt that he'd kept this power from Lea on purpose.

"If you hadn't touched an item with such a strong memory that had been locked away for so long, it might have been decades before you even realized you had this power. If ever."

"So what makes this stone so special?" she asked.

"I think I can answer that," I said. "I think we were watching that older witch turn the younger one into a hunter." I nodded toward the pile of bones and rags. "This hunter."

"I think you're right," Andros said. "The stone must have been imbued with a very dark spell that somehow enabled the transition."

"What I don't understand is why I got to see the memory, too," I said.

"Because Lea touched you," Andros said. "And once I realized, or guessed, what was happening, I grabbed Lea's arm to join the two of you inside the memory."

"Wait, you touched me after the memory began? Lea asked. "So our bodies didn't actually go anywhere?"

Andros shook his head. "No, you were here the entire time."

She looked around the cave with wonder. "It really felt like we had traveled."

"You did in a way," he said. "Just not in a traditional sense."

"It's been a big day," I said, watching Lea once again fall back against me when she tried to stand. "I think we should think about heading back to the village for now."

"That's a good idea," Andros said. "Lea may need a few days to recover from using such a strong burst of magic like this."

"I'll gather some of the others to help me clear out this cave and bring these books and items to the village so we can study them," Ourelia said.

Andros stared down at the brittle bones of the dead hunter. "They can be killed. Portals and hunters can both be defeated.

Just knowing it and seeing it with our own eyes gives us all new hope. This is a big day for The Resistance."

I left them there to clear out the cave while I carried an exhausted Lea back to the village. She slept most of the way, leaving me to focus on the memory we'd seen. There was something about it that kept nagging at me, but I couldn't quite figure it out.

It wasn't until long after I'd settled Lea into her bed that it finally hit me.

Even though we hadn't been able to hear what the two witches in the memory were saying to each other, some part of my brain had registered this one fact.

The young woman in the memory had said the older woman's name several times.

She'd called her Priestess Winter.

THIS PASSAGE

THE YEAR THAT followed was one of the most productive and important in the building of the demon resistance against the Order of Shadows.

The books we'd found in the cave were, in fact, spellbooks belonging to young witches training to become a part of the Order. It took some time to learn to read the human language, but after a few months, many of us had a working knowledge of the basics.

One of the most important books we found was the hunter's own personal journal. Through it, we confirmed what we'd already suspected. The hunter used to be human. All hunters had been human witches in the Order at some point.

Her name had been Julia when she was human. She had been an initiate of the Order of Shadows just like her mother before her. She became a full member at the age of eighteen in a ritual ceremony, but unfortunately, she didn't describe what that ceremony entailed.

Did it have something to do with the portal ceremonies we had witnessed? The terrified girls that always seemed to be a part of the ceremony could very well have been eighteen. We had no way of gaging human age, but they all seemed to be very young.

When she was in her twenties, she tried to talk her younger cousin out of joining the Order of Shadows. The exact details weren't clear, but she had broken an important rule of the Order by exposing some of their darker secrets to the younger recruits. One of the girls betrayed her confidence and she was thrown into some kind of prison in the basement of the priestess who ruled over all of the blue demon gates.

Priestess Winter.

She rules over all the blue gates. She knows where my brother is.

As punishment, Priestess Winter used a special stone to strip away all of the young witch's normal powers. We guessed this was the memory we had witnessed when Lea touched the blue stone in the hunter's den.

After her powers were taken from her, they were then replaced with darker magic. Something that allowed the hunter to live here in the demon world much longer than a normal human lifespan. Their bodies decayed but they continued to live on as ghosts of a sort.

As a hunter, she was given a new name. She seemed to retain a lot of her memories, but she had no real will of her own anymore. No ability to deny the Order what they asked, and no way to redeem herself. The passages in the journal were often tinged with madness, so the information was not always easy to understand or interpret, but we were at least able to understand that all of the hunters used to be human witches who had broken the rules or angered the priestess. The hunters were banished to the shadow world and doomed to a life of solitude and madness, their only job to locate demons who were powerful enough to be used in the human world.

Unfortunately the journals still didn't help us understand just how the demons were being used by the humans. All we were able to understand was that somehow the demons were being used to provide greater power to the witches over there.

During that year of intense study, while I looked for answers that might help me find my brother, Lea practiced her ability to see the memories of the past. We spent more and more of our time apart and I think she had begun to see that there was no room in my heart—or my life—for love.

All I knew was revenge.

Andros and Ourelia continued their work with the black roses. Now that they had some of the Order's spell books, they were able to understand some of the magic behind the roses' ability to bind a demon to a specific spot. They began to experiment with the different components of the portal rituals, adding soul stones to the center of the roses. It was dangerous work—one wrong word or step could leave a demon's powers or energy trapped inside the stone forever—but what they learned was invaluable to the cause.

On this particular day, just over a year since we had discovered the abandoned portal in the cave, they both came running up to the village, their faces filled with excitement.

"You will not believe what we've discovered," Ourelia said.

"It's incredible," Andros said. "Something that will change everything."

"A portal?" I asked, my heart racing.

"Better," Andros said, smiling. "Get the others."

It took us some time to round everyone up. Especially Lea. She'd been growing more and more distant lately. When I finally found her, she was sitting alone looking out over the sea. There were storms in the distance, causing the waves to rise and fall violently. Not a calm day today.

"Andros wants to show us something important," I said. I noticed the sadness etched on her face. "Are you okay?"

She turned and gave me a strange, sad smile. "I'm okay," she said.

"Have you been out here alone all morning?" I asked.

"Let's see what Andros has to show us," she said, standing. She didn't answer my question.

Her sadness frightened me. Had she seen something in the memories of the past?

She joined me in the village. Ourelia and Andros had already gathered the rest of the group together in the village center. By this time, there were nearly two hundred of us.

"I know there has been some concern lately about our growing numbers," Andros began, addressing the crowd now that we had arrived. "We need as many demons to join our cause as possible, but since we know the king will not approve of what we are doing, we have to be careful not to draw too much attention."

"For now, we've managed to avoid his concern. All we've done is help rebuild the villages and other harmless actions," Ourelia added. "But the more we learn about the Order, the more we feel that battle is close. When that moment comes, we are going to need a safe place to hide, away from the eyes of both the king and the Order."

She glanced at Lea, who did not drop her gaze or act in any way.

"Recently, we lucked upon a very happy gift," Andros said, a smile bigger than any I'd ever seen on his face before. "A few weeks ago, while looking for a new, larger home for our camp, Ourelia and I stumbled upon the entrance to a cave."

"A very large cave," Ourelia said. They were both giggling like children. "We spent several days exploring the area to make sure it was safe and uninhabited. You are not going to believe this place."

"You'll have to see for yourself to understand the magnitude of this discovery," Andros said. "But I think we've found a new home for The Resistance."

They led us through the Obsidian Forest and across a small stream to a clearing in the woods. In the center of the clearing was a ring of black roses. Confused, I turned to Andros.

"I thought you said you found a cave. This looks like one of the Order's portals," I said.

Andros smiled. "That's the other big surprise," he said. "Through my experiments with the roses, I was able to develop a security system of sorts. Ourelia and I spent the last week covering the original entrance to the caves with this new door."

"How does it work?" Lea asked.

"When the black roses and the soul stones are used together, they can pull a demon into a circle and hold them there," he said. "This is how the order uses the magic. But I learned that if I put roses on both sides, I could actually turn this into more of a doorway. A passage, allowing a demon to enter one side and come out the other. It's like a portal of sorts, but since we control the magic, we can also control who can enter."

"And it's safe?" Azira asked, wringing her hands together.

"Completely," Andros said. "I'll prove it."

He stepped into the circle of roses and his body disappeared. The crowd around us gasped.

I looked to Ourelia. "Where did he go?"

"He's inside the cave below us now," she said. "Trust us."

She motioned for me to enter the circle, but I was afraid. It wasn't that I didn't trust Andros. It was just more of a fear of the unknown. I had no idea how Andros had figured out the way the roses worked, but what if he was wrong?

Lea stepped forward and took my hand in hers. It had been months since we'd touched and the feel of her skin on mine surprised me.

"We'll go together," she said.

I nodded and squeezed her hand. Together, we walked into the center of the roses.

She put her arms tight around my waist and drew in a surprised gasp as the roses pulled us through, our forms turning to smoke and tumbling around as we were pulled through the solid earth.

It was a feeling of separating from myself. Not quite like turning to my shadow form. Even in shadows, I am whole. I cannot turn invisible and walk through walls.

This was more like being taken apart and put back together again.

When we pushed through to the darkness of the cave below, I took a deep breath and held Lea to my body. Her breath came fast and her chest rose and fell against my own. She looked up at me with such a mix of adoration and longing that it broke my heart into pieces.

She deserved to be loved. She deserved so much more than this. Tears filled my eyes and I wanted so badly to tell her the truth. That someone did love her. That it was all my fault he was gone.

Even after all these years, I could not forgive myself for his disappearance.

And I could not love her the way he'd asked me to.

It suddenly felt as if this brief journey—this passage through the earth and into the darkness of the cave below—was a sign of times to come. This embrace was the beginning of the end somehow, although at the time I couldn't explain how or why I knew it. But I sensed it with all that I was. We were on the edge of great change.

And I think she knew it too.

I looked away and released my hold on her. Lea's shoulders fell and her eyes darkened. The moment of tenderness between us passed as quickly as it had come. Never to come again.

THE UNDERGROUND

*W*ORDS CANNOT DESCRIBE the awe we all felt as the small corridor emptied out into a large hall. I had never seen an underground cave with such extensive carvings and gemstones.

The hall itself was dirty and needed a lot of work to bring it back to its former glory, but it was breath-taking even in its run-down state. The ceilings in the Grand Hall were as high as the sky. It reached out so far it was difficult to even see the back of the hallway from the stairs here at the entrance.

Smooth white marble, unlike anything I'd ever seen before, adorned the floors. Tall circular columns rose up from the ground, reaching all the way to the ceiling, adorned with intricate patterns of gold. Grand staircases curved down either side of the entrance, leading down to the floor of the Grand Hall.

Six smaller staircases on each side of the Grand Hall each led up to their own separate corridors. Just how big was this place? And who did it belong to?

"What is this place?" I whispered.

Andros stepped toward me as I stared out over the main balcony, my eyes drinking in the enormity of the hall. "This is the palace of the Troll King."

I laughed, not believing him at first. But when I turned to look at him, I realized he wasn't kidding.

My smile faded, replaced with an open jaw and wide eyes. "You're kidding me," I said. "Trolls are real?"

He leaned against the railing. "Were," he said. "As far as we can tell, they're extinct now. Possibly for several thousand years."

"How do you know it belonged to the trolls?" Lea asked.

Andros smiled. "Besides the incredible size of this place? There's a library," he said. "Come on, let me show you guys around."

The ancient troll caves proved to be the perfect place for The Resistance. We called it the Underground, and it fit in every way.

With the amazing amount of space deep inside the caves, we had all the room we would ever need to not only train an army but also to protect those who would seek shelter inside our walls. Several of the corridors off the main hall held hundreds of rooms, which we each claimed for our own homes. There was a library like Andros had said, full of floor-to-ceiling bookcases made out of white marble. Most of the books inside were written in an ancient language none of us could speak, but we claimed this as the home of our research on the Order as well.

At the back of the Grand Hall, we found rooms that were perfect for training our army, including one that was large enough to hold over a hundred soldiers all running tactics at once.

Together, we fortified the spells and traps at the entrance to the Underground. There was no way the Order—or even the king—could come inside without one of us opening the door and inviting them inside. It was the safest place in the kingdom next to the throne room itself.

Andros proved to be a great leader during those years. He appointed a council of members to lead. Ourelia was in charge of recruiting new soldiers and residents. Azira had taken on the task of organizing the library. Jericho was put in charge of security, building a team of trusted recruits to guard the entrance day and night.

Lea, Andros, and I took turns teaching battle skills to the newer recruits.

Andros also took on the task of organizing the layout of the Underground. He assigned demons to their homes and turned the Grand Hall into a gathering place and a market.

The Underground—and The Resistance—thrived. It became home to more than a thousand demons in its first five years alone. Some of those thousand were trained as warriors, ready to fight against the Order if it came to that. Others were children and elders who became part of the community and who blossomed in the security and safety of the caves.

The demons of The Resistance began to speak of Lea and me as the future hope of the kingdom. They spoke of a time when the king would give his throne to his daughter and how we would restore the kingdom to its former glory. For them, we kept up the appearance of a couple who would someday be married, but we kept separate residences and rarely spoke of anything beyond the business of running the Underground city. Over the years, her sadness turned to cold determination.

It was a time of great change and great progress. The others were concentrating on building something powerful, but on the inside, I was falling apart. At night in the solitude of my room, I spent all my time reading through spellbooks, maps, and journals, retreating farther into myself with each day that passed. I drew pictures of my visions and memorized every single detail of every ritual I'd observed.

I needed to know. I needed to understand what had happened. There had to be a clue in there somewhere. I had to be missing something. So I relived it. Not a moment went by that I wasn't thinking of revenge or regret.

FORGIVE ME

It had been close to fifty years since Aerden had disappeared when the knock on my door that would change everything came.

I had been inside my small room in the Underground, drawing again. It was very late at night, but I hadn't been sleeping much. So much time had passed since Aerden had been taken that I had started to lose hope of ever seeing him alive again. All that held me to this hope was a single vision I'd had of him recently. He was standing in front of me, his form black and strange, his eyes distant. What did it mean?

And when would I see him again? How did I know this vision was real and not some random wish of an obsessed mind?

I had started to lose myself, thinking that if there was no hope of ever seeing my brother again, what was I living for at all?

Revenge? We'd been planning revenge for decades, but we never fought back. All this training was worth nothing if we weren't prepared to fight.

Despite our growth in power and numbers, Andros still refused to begin the war against the Order.

He preached patience, saying that demons had been around a lot longer than humans. He said demons were immortal while humans were fragile. We had time, he would say.

But I wasn't so sure. To me, he sounded like the King of the North with his assurances that because we were immortal, we were stronger than the humans.

Why couldn't they see that while we were being patient, the Order was growing stronger? The longer we waited the less chance we had of ever defeating them.

With each passing year, I felt Aerden slipping away from me. I felt my memories of him fading.

And it was tearing me apart. When I wasn't training, I spent almost all of my time alone in my room or wandering the outerlands, looking for portals. I hardly spoke to anyone, because I had nothing to talk about. All I thought about was Aerden and all I dreamed about was revenge.

Then, one night, a timid knock sounded on my door.

I'd been in the middle of an intricate drawing, immersed in my thoughts of killing Priestess Winter someday. The interruption was an annoyance. Who would be coming to visit me this late at night?

I yanked the door open, scowling and ready to tear into whoever had disturbed me so late.

But it was Lea. And the look on her face scared me.

She'd been crying, and these days, Lea simply didn't cry. She hadn't shown much emotion at all in years, come to think of it. Training the Resistance army and rising up as a leader of the Underground had hardened her.

"What is it?" I asked.

"There's something I need to show you," she said. Her voice wasn't much more than a whisper.

"Is everything okay?" I glanced down the long corridor, wondering if someone had upset her. But the place was empty and quiet, everyone asleep in their rooms.

"Yes," she said. A tear fell across her cheek. "No. I don't know."

I knew I should comfort her. Put my arms around her. But the time for that kind of affection between us had long passed. I didn't want to be close to her. Or anyone. I just wanted to be left alone.

"Whatever it is, it's going to be okay," I said, wondering what had her so upset. "We'll face it together."

"Will we?" she asked. A sob escaped her lips and she turned from me, holding her hand up to hide the sound of her cries.

I stepped forward and placed a hand on her shoulders and she jumped in surprise, as if I had burned her. I moved my hand away quickly.

"What did you want to show me?" I asked. "Maybe it will help when I see for myself."

She shook her head. "It will help you," she said. "That's the only reason I'm showing you after all this time. But it will not help me. It will only take you farther from me. But I see now that it's the only way."

I didn't understand what she meant at first. Her words were a mystery, but she didn't say anything more until she had led me down the quiet corridor, through the Grand Hall, and out into the evening air.

We traveled in complete silence, through the Obsidian Forest, along quiet roads and empty fields until we had come to a place near the Black Cliffs. The king's city rose up against the night sky in the distance on one side while the cliffs gave way to the Sea of Glass on the other.

"Why have you brought me so far out here?" I asked. It had taken hours for us to get here and the moons were very low in the night sky.

Her green eyes darkened and chills swept across my skin.

And I knew without a word from her. She wanted to show me a memory. An important memory.

My hands shook as I reached for her. Sorrow and hope both warred in my heart, squeezing it until I couldn't take it any longer. I opened my mouth to catch my breath.

She took my hands tentatively at first, only touching her fingertips to mine, as if she were still uncertain. Then, finally, she slid her fingers down the length of my fingers and wrapped them around mine until they were entwined so tightly I could barely tell them apart.

"I hope you'll forgive me," she said.

"For what?" I asked. The wind blowing off the cliffs carried my voice away.

"For keeping this from you for so long." She closed her eyes and took several deep breaths. The sky around us darkened and then disappeared as we shook and tumbled and fell. When everything settled, I opened my eyes and looked around at a familiar scene.

A scene that stopped my heart inside my chest and brought me to my knees.

We were standing inside the memory of the moment Aerden was taken from this world.

MY BROTHER'S PAIN

MY BROTHER STOOD in front of me, his eyes unseeing. I stood and called out his name, but he could not hear me.

Like before, the memory was slightly dull in color, but the vision was clear. I reached out for him, accidentally letting go of Lea's hands. But somehow, inside the memory itself, it didn't seem to matter that we weren't touching.

I reached for my brother, out of my mind with regret and sorrow. I wanted nothing more than to be able to grab onto him and take him from this place. I would have given anything to change the events of that day.

If I could have, I would have traded places with him in an instant. It should have been him standing in the throne room with Lea all those years ago. I should have insisted he tell her the truth so that he could take my place and claim her as his own.

But this was only a memory. I reached for Aerden, but my hands went straight through him as if he were no more than a ghost.

A beautiful human woman with long white-blond hair stood in front of him. She wore a beautiful blue velvet robe adorned with silver embroidery. She smiled at him and ran a hand along his cheek.

"You have no idea how glad I am that you came," she said. Her voice was muffled inside the memory, but easy to understand. Lea must have done a lot of work on her skill to make the voice as clear as it was. "I know your heart is broken now, but I promise you that you will find a new home in my world. It will be a place where your power and your light will be used in such amazing ways."

I paced around him, screaming for him to run away, but it was no use. Watching him fall into this trap made me feel weaker and more useless than I'd ever felt in my life.

"I'm ready," he said.

The woman held her hand out to him. "I have something for you first," she said. "A gift."

He opened his hand and returned her smile. I stared down in anticipation, powerless to stop these events from happening. The woman dropped something into his hand and closed his fist around it. At first, I couldn't quite make out what it was, but I saw its effect immediately.

Aerden's face tensed and his entire arm shook as the object in his hand paralyzed him. I could feel his intense struggle against the black magic, but it was already too late. His fist was closed around the item, but a silver chain dangled from it—delicate and beautiful.

My brother's eyes searched the face of the witch, then widened in horror as she transformed from a beautiful young girl to an old woman and then, finally, to an entirely different woman. It was difficult for me to judge age, but this third form seemed to be in the middle of the other two—not too old and not too young. All three of her appearances were similar in their coloring with white hair and the same piercing light blue eyes, almost as if she had cycled through generations of the same family, transforming from younger daughter to grandmother to mother.

Her smile grew dark and twisted as she stared at Aerden's horror.

"I love this moment," she said, moving her face so close to him their cheeks were nearly touching. "The moment when a powerful demon like you realizes for the first time that he has made a very terrible mistake."

Aerden struggled to speak, but it was no use. Whatever was in his hand had him completely trapped for the moment, unable to move or speak or fight.

The witch laughed and the sound tore its way through my soul. She was enjoying this. My brother's pain was amusing to her.

I curled my hands into claws and ripped at where her heart should be, but my hands only touched air. Nothingness.

"I didn't lie, you know," she said. "You were chosen for a very important purpose and your sacrifice here today will never be forgotten. Your power will be used, I promise you. You're one of the lucky ones, really. You'll learn to thank me eventually. As the demon of a prima, you'll live much longer than the others."

She released his hand, but his fist stayed closed around the object she'd put inside. She walked around him, whispering in his ear.

"But I may have lied about how much you'll enjoy your time in my world," she said. "I'm afraid it's not going to be very pleasant. Especially this next part. The less you struggle against it, the better it will be. Trust me."

Something shimmered inside her blue robe as she reached her hand inside. I gasped as she pulled out a dagger made of a silver metal that I recognized. A metal that comes from our own world, just like the gemstones she used.

She placed the tip of the blade against Aerden's back and I cringed, tears flowing down my face. I couldn't bear to see him hurt. This was torture.

She ran the blade across his flesh, from his back to his shoulder and around to his neck. She cut a very thin slice into his neck and his blood poured from it, black at first, then turning to a deep blue. She quickly pulled a silver cup adorned with blue stones from her robe and collected the blood inside as Aerden struggled to pull away. I could see the sheer terror in his eyes.

From the corner of my eye, movement drew my attention. I turned to see a robed figure floating up from the edge of the Black Cliffs. She wore a robe that had been torn into rags. When she lifted her head, I could see that part of her face had begun to decay.

A hunter.

But not so far gone as most of the ones I had seen in the portal rituals I'd witnessed over the years. This was a fresh hunter.

"Yanora," the witch said. "Are you ready to be bound to this portal?"

The hunter nodded, as if she had a choice, but I knew she had none. Dark magic bound her to obey.

"Yes, Priestess Winter."

My gaze snapped toward the woman. Priestess Winter, ruler of the blue portals. She had betrayed my brother.

This woman did not look the same as the woman I had seen in the previous memory, when Lea had first taken us into that hallway to watch the hunter being drained with the stone. She did not have the same face, but she had the same name.

Anger surged through me. See? It didn't matter that the humans were not immortal. They may not live more than a hundred years, but they had powerful traditions. They were passing their knowledge down through the generations, training their daughters and their granddaughters to take over when they died.

The king was ignorant to believe we could outlast them simply because we were immortal.

His ignorance would be the end of us all.

"Bind him," the priestess commanded.

Yanora, the hunter, floated toward my brother, then bound his hands and legs in shackles with sharp spikes along the inside. Blue blood ran from his wrists and ankles as she locked them in.

Priestess Winter forced his fist open, revealing to me for the first time a silver pendant with a bright blue stone inside, its chain dangling from his hand. She took it from him and placed it inside the cup of his blood.

With the necklace gone, Aerden regained some small ability to move. He screamed and fought against the shackles, but the pain of the spikes kept him from shifting to smoke. The hunter held fast to his chains and cast something to bind his mouth.

"It isn't any use struggling," Priestess Winter told him, her voice harsh. "You belong to me now."

She laid the items in the grass at his feet. A dagger. A cup. A necklace. A ring. Each with a single blue stone embedded in the silver.

Then, she knelt at his feet and began to chant. She lifted her palms toward the sky and as she spoke, black-thorned vines rose up through the dark rock, shattering it to pieces. The wind carried it away like dust, leaving a small clearing of earth that looked as though it had been burned. The vines grew up in a perfect circle, then stopped. Slowly, the tips grew buds as black as night that blossomed into roses, their petals opening to the stormy sky above.

Priestess Winter continued to chant as the sky cracked with lightning. She looked up, surprised. There was fear in her eyes.

"You should not be able to cast," she said. She stood and checked the shackles at his wrist. More lightning sounded above, then cracked to earth, a burst of fire erupting where it landed.

"Hurry," she shouted to Yanora. What was fear at first, transformed to excitement and awe. The corners of her mouth curled up into a smile that sent a terrible chill down my spine. "He's stronger than we ever dreamed."

The pair of them rushed into place, continuing their chants.

I knew I should pay attention to the ritual, but all I could do was stare at my brother's face. His pain and terror cut through me. I should have been there to save him. I should have gone looking for him the moment I realized he was gone that morning.

"I'm so sorry," I shouted to him, even though I knew he couldn't hear me.

My brother fell to his knees amongst the roses, their thorns tearing into his flesh. He cried out, sobbing with such heart-shattering pain that I almost lost myself to madness.

"No," I shouted. I threw myself to the ground at his knees, not wanting to see this but knowing I must.

Lea, who had been standing in silence at the edge of the memory, came to sit beside me, her body shaking with tears. She put her hand on my arm as we watched the blue light begin to pool in the center of the circle.

The light nearly blinded me, but I clutched at Aerden's form, trying desperately to pull him back as he began to shift from solid to smoky blackness.

A disturbance rocked the scene as a demon raced forward. My heart stopped. I had seen this part before.

I forced myself to sit up and watch; wanting to make sense of the pieces of this I had seen on the day Aerden was taken.

The demon rushed forward, sword drawn. He sliced through the black roses at Aerden's knees and miraculously, the blue light of the portal disappeared. But only for an instant. It was like a flash.

Priestess Winter lost her concentration only for an instant. With a single motion of her wrist, she brought the intruding demon to his knees. She nodded to the hunter, who then took a shiny black soul stone from the pocket of her rags and pressed it to his palm. His body shifted to smoke then was sucked into the stone, screaming as his life force was sucked from his body and locked inside the stone.

I looked away, horrified. This was a process that was sacred in my culture—reserved for the respected passing of an elder. A choice that is made in sacrifice and love. Not a murderous weapon to be used to steal souls. My hatred for this witch and her Order of Shadows grew so great within me that I nearly lost my mind. A fearsome, painful cry ripped from my throat. The Order of Shadows had taken our gems, our silver, our traditions, and turned them against us as weapons of dark magic.

I wanted to make every witch who ever lived pay for this betrayal. This absolute corruption of all I held sacred.

Hatred consumed me.

I watched as the black roses regrew themselves to reform the circle. Priestess Winter resumed her chanting and the blue pool of light formed again.

She stood and stepped through the light, lifting her hood over her face as she moved between worlds.

Just as in the other rituals, the light inside the portal was too bright for me to see everything on the other side. All I could make out was a young girl inside, her hair in braids. Instead of hovering over the light, she was kneeling, a white gown pooling on the floor around her.

She looked up, her brown eyes startled as she saw the demon bound and shackled on the other side. She looked up to question the priestess, but it was too late for questions.

The priestess secured the blue pendant around the girl's neck.

I turned to my brother. I was beyond tears now, knowing the moment was close. I was destroyed, madness and rage consuming me as I clawed at his ghostly form.

For a moment, he briefly opened his eyes and looked almost straight at me. He seemed to understand something about what was happening to him. Something I had still not grasped. He managed to say one word before his body turned to smoke and was sucked through the portal of blue light.

"Denaer," he said, then was gone.

EMERALDS
THE HUMAN WORLD, PRESENT DAY

I RELEASED MY GRIP on the memory stone, letting it drop to the wooden boards of the front porch.

I leaned forward and dropped my head into my hands, unable to control the flood of tears. These memories were the most difficult, and I knew they would be hard for Harper to see, too. After all, that had been her ancestor sitting on the floor of that ritual room, waiting to become Prima.

I stood and wiped my tears against the sleeve of my white shirt. I walked over to the window and looked inside, careful to stay hidden in the shadows on the porch. I didn't want anyone to see me like this, but I had to know it was real.

I had to know that my brother was alive and safe.

Aerden stood on the other side of the room. His laughter carried all the way out here and the sound warmed the chill in my heart.

I watched him, still hardly able to believe we were both here. Both safe after all this time. After all these years of struggle and hopelessness.

I still couldn't believe Priestess Winter was gone. I'd never hated someone so much, but she had seemed so strong. Untouchable.

But Harper had come along and changed everything. She had shown us that you can't ever give up, even when there doesn't seem to be any hope left.

Without her, none of this would have been possible.

But she was right. We still had so much work to do. There were still four more sisters to defeat. Thousands of portals to close.

And we still didn't know the first thing about the mysterious High Priestess who ruled over them all.

Harper and I, along with the rest of the newly formed Demon Liberation Movement, had spent a lot of time since the defeat of Priestess Winter discussing which sister we would go after next.

We had some information about the priestess who ruled over the red portals, but it was the green portals I wanted next. I didn't care that we had no real leads or clues as to how to find the priestess who controlled the emerald stones. I just knew that second to blue, green was the one who had hurt the people I loved most.

Andros and I may not have agreed on how to handle the witches of the Order of Shadows, but despite our differences, I owed him this after all he had done for me. Andros and Ourelia had both lost loved ones to emerald portals.

Harper agreed with me about the emeralds. Her friends from Cypress, Prima Sullivan and her daughters Caroline and Meredith, were bound to the Order still. They wanted to be free just as we were now free. And because of what had happened when Harper had saved Caroline from the crow witch, there was a piece of Cypress's demon locked inside of Harper. She felt a duty to free him.

Lea and Aerden both felt that red was a better target since we knew more about it, but in the end, the decision was Harper's to make.

Emerald would be next.

I looked through the window at the party going on inside and soaked in the sounds of happiness. Laughter. Music. Footsteps dancing across the hardwoods. If I could have, I would have bottled that happiness and taken it back in time with me to the day I had to face that dark memory. I would have told my younger self that even though the darkest of times lay just ahead, there was hope of better days.

Harper had taught me that.

There is always hope.

I made my way back to the steps of the front porch and sat down on the top step. I picked up the discarded memory stone and held it tight in my fist. I was almost finished, but the rest of my journey to Peachville was the most difficult part.

As much as I wanted to put off the memories of what came next, I was running out of time. I had to talk to Harper tonight. I had to finish this and give it to Harper before tomorrow came.

Because I had seen the future.

And tomorrow would be too late.

YOU WERE ALREADY BROKEN

THE SHADOW WORLD, 51 YEARS AGO

WHEN THE MEMORY had faded and our minds had returned to the field of black rock, Lea held me close and let me weep. I moved between rage and sorrow, tearing at my clothes one minute and sobbing the next.

It took me a long time to calm myself, but Lea waited patiently, never leaving my side.

Finally, she touched my arm.

"I'm sorry you had to see that," she said. "But I know you needed to see so that you could understand."

I nodded, my throat raw from screaming, my eyelids heavy and tired.

"I can't even imagine what kind of torture he has been through," I said. "He didn't deserve that."

"No," she said softly. "No one deserves that."

I clenched my jaw and my lips trembled. "Priestess Winter and the witches she commands deserve that and worse," I said.

"They can't be allowed to continue this madness. We have to stop them."

The words were passionate, but I had no energy left to shout them. I felt weak, trapped between a strong desire for vengeance and an ignorance of how to achieve it.

I remembered then what Lea had said to me just before she showed me the memory. She said to forgive her for taking this long to show it to me.

"How long have you known about this memory?" I asked. "When did you come by it?"

Her eyes fluttered closed and she looked away, toward the cliffs where the suns had begun to rise.

"Almost twenty years ago," she said. "The day Andros showed us the troll caves."

I nodded, my heart in so much pain I was numb to it. "The day I found you sitting by these cliffs alone," I said.

"Yes."

"Why did you wait?"

"Because I was afraid it would break you," she said. She opened her eyes and stared straight into me. "I was afraid that if you saw this memory, every hope I had of a future with you would die forever and that you would be lost to pain and rage."

Tears gathered in her eyes, then cascaded down her face like a waterfall of sorrow.

"Only, the problem is, I think I lost you a long time ago. I was just too blind to see it," she said. Her chest hitched with each breath. She reached a hand out toward my arm, but then drew it back. "The light of love in your heart stone was the brightest, most brilliant light of my life. I have always loved you, Denaer, but I never dreamed you could love me back. You have no idea how hard it has been for me the past fifty years. To know your love only for an instant before you reclaimed it."

She brought her fist to her chest and clutched at her shirt, then lowered her head, resting it on her fist as she cried.

"I thought that maybe if I was patient and waited by your side, you would come to realize that I was more important to you than your brother," she said. "And I know that's horrible because how could I mean as much to you as he does?" She lifted her eyes to mine again and they sparkled with the drops of a thousand tears. "God, how I have wanted you to love me the way I love you. I have waited for the bright love I saw in that heart stone to shine through your eyes when you looked at me. I would give anything to know, just for one more moment, that you loved me. But whatever they did to you—and to Aerden—stole that from me. From both of us. I've been a fool to believe we could go back to the way things might have been. I was afraid the memory of this ritual would break you, but I know now that you were already broken. You've been broken since the moment they ripped him from this world. All that is left for me is to let you go."

I reached for her hand and brought it to my lips in a soft kiss.

"I'm sorry," I whispered.

I was so incredibly sorry. I never intended to cause her this pain. All I had ever wanted was to do the right thing by everyone. By my country, my parents, my brother. I wanted to make everyone else happy. But in the end, following your heart is the only way to happiness, even if it means disappointing those around you.

It was a lesson I would have to learn many times before I really came to understand it.

Lea lifted her hand to my cheek and wiped away my tears. She straightened her shoulders and when she looked at me again, I saw that something inside her hand changed tonight. She seemed resolved. As if her moment of weakness had given birth to a new kind of strength.

"Come with me," she said, her voice still raw but strong. "I'll take you to the portal."

I'VE CARRIED IT WITH ME

I CALLED AN EMERGENCY meeting of the council as soon as we returned to the Underground.

"What's happened?" Ourelia asked.

Andros, Ourelia, Azira, Jericho, Lea and I all took our places around a large wooden table in the library. We'd been meeting here to discuss plans for training and organizing for years, but in my mind, this was the single most important meeting we'd ever had. I needed them to be with me on this.

And if they weren't, I would go alone.

"I have found the portal where my brother was taken," I said.

Azira gasped, then clamped a hand over her mouth.

Andros swallowed, his eyes darting toward Ourelia for a moment. They looked more worried than excited, and I knew before they even said a word that they did not want to help me fight.

I pressed my lips together tightly to keep from saying something I might regret.

"The portal is near the Black Cliffs," Lea said. "Not too far from the king's city, among the fields of black stone."

Azira's mouth was slightly open. She shook her head in wonder. "All this time and it was right there?" she asked. "How did we miss it? We must have searched that area a thousand times."

"It's very difficult to see the black roses among the rocks," I said. "The entire clearing blends in so well, you have to be standing almost directly on top of it to notice it. Lea's the one who found it."

I didn't mention how long ago she had found the portal because thinking about her keeping this a secret for so long made me feel ill and unsettled. I understood why she did it, but that didn't make it any easier to accept.

"I discovered the memory of the portal some time ago," she said. "I had an item of Aerden's I had kept with me and I spent some of my memory training traveling to different locations throughout the kingdom and concentrating on his memory."

I turned. She hadn't mentioned this to me when we were alone. "What item?"

She brought a silver key from her pocket and placed it on the table. She ran her finger across the top of it. "Aerden gave me this key a few days before he disappeared," she said. She didn't look up at me. This was another secret she had kept from me. "He wouldn't even tell me what it went to. He only said it was important for me to keep it. That it would keep me safe. I didn't think much of it until after he was gone, but I've carried it with me ever since."

I leaned over and picked up the key, turning it over in my hand. It was a small key with a long, slender stem. The top of the key was adorned with a set of intricate knots, a small clear stone set in the center. Was it enchanted?

I handed it back to her, wondering why she had kept it a secret all this time.

What other secrets had she been keeping?

"It took me a long time, but one day, there it was. The memory of him being taken," she said. "It was very weak at first. I could barely make out the events of the day and I couldn't hear anything they were saying. But over time, the closer I moved to the portal itself, the stronger the memory became."

"That must have been very difficult for you to see," Azira said, concern etched on her face.

"It was necessary," I said. "The ritual the Order performed when Aerden was taken was different from the other rituals we've seen."

I reached for a tattered book I had found among the hunter's belongings inside the cave. I flipped through the pages until I found what I'd been looking for, then opened it completely and slid it across the table toward Andros.

"This passage describes the prima. We already knew she was the one who led the rituals at each portal. In this book it says that prima means first. The first demon pulled through the portal, somehow bound to the first witch," I said. "It doesn't explain how they are bound, but it seems to be some type of slavery where the witch is using the demon's essence to fuel her own magic. The prima is created at the same time the portal itself is created. This matches up with what we saw with Aerden. When the ritual began, there were no roses and there was no portal. At first, there was the witch—Priestess Winter—who we already know is connected to all of the blue portals. She performed the ritual which then opened this particular portal for the first time."

Andros and Ourelia poured over the book I'd passed to them.

Finally Andros looked up from the page. "And you believe Aerden was one of these firsts?" he asked. "That he is a prima?"

"Yes," I said. "Either that or he is somehow tied to the prima. We won't know the exact hierarchy until we are able to get over there and see it for ourselves."

"Wait a moment," Andros said, standing. "We can't send anyone over there. It would be suicide without an army to back them up."

"Maybe not." I lifted my palm, wanting him to just hear me out. I had been working on a plan for years and even though I knew Andros was against fighting the Order until we had more information about their weaknesses, I felt there was a way around it. "What if we were able to go through for only a few minutes? What if we could guarantee a small amount of time on the other side without anyone being in real danger? We could get a look at the other side. We could see what the witches are doing and whether they are keeping the demons there in the portal room. If Aerden's there—"

"How would we ever be able to guarantee anyone's safety while they were over there? Not to mention those of us here on the other side. If the witches saw us, what would keep the hunter and the witches inside the portal from coming after us? This is madness," Ourelia said.

"In the memory of Aerden's disappearance, I saw a demon rush forward. A demon wearing a red dragon on his armband just like yours," I said, motioning toward the band on Andros' arm. It was his family's insignia and one that had become a symbol of The Resistance. "You said you knew that demon."

"Mirabi."

"Yes. He must have seen the ritual taking place and rushed forward to try to help," I said. "I don't know why he chose to act. Maybe it was because this ritual was different from the others. Maybe he recognized Aerden. We'll never know for sure. But when he interrupted the ritual, he used his sword to cut down some of the black roses. Immediately, the blue light of the portal disappeared, as if the magic of the portal couldn't work without the roses."

Andros studied me. "What are you proposing?"

I went through my plan and everyone listened quietly. When I was finished, I felt certain they would agree to help me. This was my chance to save my brother. Or if not save him, at least to get enough information about the witches holding him captive that we could come up with a better, stronger plan for rescuing him later.

"Aerden's alive over there," I said. "I just want a few moments to get a better look at the other side."

Ourelia shook her head. "I don't think we're ready for something like this," she said. "If we attack them or show any kind of aggressive behavior, they are going to send hunters after us. Or other human witches. We don't understand their magic enough to defeat them."

"Bullshit," I said, my anger ruling me. "We've done nothing but talk and learn and try to understand for decades now. When is it going to be time to fight back? How will we learn to fight them if we don't actually fight? It's the best way to learn. Andros, you know that. You're the one who taught me that. We have to fight in order to learn how to fight better."

Andros nodded. "Yes, I know I said that, but we've got so much at stake right now," he said. "We've built this entire Underground to keep people safe. If we start a battle now, before we're really ready, we risk putting them all in danger."

"The only reason these demons need a safe place to live is because the Order of Shadows has made their homelands unsafe," I said. "Hiding a thousand demons in caves is no different from the king himself hiding away inside his gated city."

Andros lowered his head to his hands. He knew I was right. They couldn't hide here forever. Yes, it would be hard to lose anyone, but wars meant loss.

They also meant fighting for freedom.

"We have to do something. We can't just sit here in the safety of these caves for the rest of our days," I said. "It won't make any real difference because out there, the Order will still be stealing demons from their homes and turning them into slaves."

"I agree with you," Ourelia said. "There will come a time when we have to stand and fight, but it's not that time yet. I know you want to save your brother, but what chance will you really have of saving him? We don't know the first thing about what goes on in the human world."

"And how do you think we're ever going to find out?" I asked. "The only way is to go over there ourselves and get the answers we seek."

"I agree with Denaer," Jericho said. It was the first time he had spoken since we first gathered together in the library. "I think it's worth a shot. We don't have to start a fight or even attack anyone. We just send someone through to gather information and then bring them back."

"We all know who would go through," Azira said, looking to me. "I think losing you is too much of a risk right now. Maybe we should spend a few years gathering more information about this particular portal. If we could observe a few of their rituals, maybe we could find out something specific about the witches who operate that portal."

I shook my head. I couldn't wait years. I had already waited far too long.

I listened to the others argue and debate, trying to look patient and understanding. But inside, I was losing my mind. How could we even be debating this? After fifty long years, I finally knew where my brother was. There was no way I would sit back and watch while more demons were pulled through that portal. For what? Research?

Screw research. We had done enough watching and waiting.

It was time to act.

"Denaer?" Lea's voice pulled me from my thoughts. I had been sitting with my head cupped between my hands, shaking my head furiously from side-to-side.

I realized now everyone was watching me. Waiting to hear what I would have to say.

I swallowed, looking to her with questions in my eyes.

She gave me a sad smile. "I'm sorry," she said. "The council agrees that we need more time. More information."

I sat back, then studied the faces of my friends sitting around the table. My heart filled with sorrow and rage. I had no words. No final plea. They had already heard what I had to say and they had still decided against me.

I placed my hands flat against the top of the table as ice gathered on my fingertips. I stood, then shook my head.

I slammed my hand down on the table and ice cracked like glass, shattering and spraying in all directions across the top of the table. I turned and shifted, leaving the room before anyone could stop by. I felt completely abandoned.

I had nothing more to say to them. If they wouldn't help me, I would have to go alone.

IMPOSSIBLE

I FLEW THROUGH THE tall corridor, wanting to go straight to the portal and charge through. I wanted to force them to give my brother back to me.

But I knew that was impossible.

I couldn't save my brother simply by force of will. These witches weren't going to hand him over simply because I asked. But knowing where he was, how could I live another minute without going after him?

The floor iced over as I passed, frost spreading up the wall like growing vines.

I flew toward the only place where I knew I could let out my frustration without hurting anyone. The training rooms.

The training hall was empty this time of morning and I went into the first room, slamming the door behind me. I lifted Aerden's axe from the strap across my back and initiated the battle sequence Lea had set up. One of her abilities was to create illusions of warriors. We had used these illusions to simulate real battles. That was Andros' idea. He'd been saying from the beginning that a great warrior was best trained by fighting great opponents.

So why was he so hesitant to fight against the Order?

How were we ever going to become great warriors if we were too afraid to face them? How would we ever make a difference?

The battle illusions began and four witches appeared in the different corners of the room.

I focused my rage on their human faces, wanting to destroy every human that ever lived. Wanting to wipe them from existence for their evil. I lifted the axe and flew through the air, gathering my power in my hands so that the entire axe became encased in a thick layer of cold blue ice. I approached the witch from above, bringing my weapon down on her head, splitting her in two. The illusion fell to the floor, then vanished.

I holstered the axe and turned to the second witch, shifting to smoke as she set her eyes on me and cast a spell that would have paralyzed me. I snaked around the edges of the room, finding a stretch of shadows to hide inside before coming around behind her. I reformed before she even had time to turn toward me, then placed both of my hands on her shoulders. As a human, she had no ability to shift and slip from my grip.

I took a deep breath in, gathering hatred from my heart before blowing the air back out toward the back of her head. She only had time to slightly angle her head toward me before her body froze, ice crystals forming on her pale skin. I moved around in front of her, then clenched my hand into a fist. With all my strength, I punched her in the center of her stomach. A loud crack echoed in the training room as I hit my mark perfectly. Tiny cracks spread out from the larger one where my fist had hit.

I flipped around, kicking my foot into her side. The witch shattered into a thousand pieces that scattered across the floor.

The final two witches sent their assaults toward me, one sending a ball of fire toward my head while the other attempted to bring the ceiling down on top of me. Focused on vengeance,

I shifted easily, moving out of the way as a large chunk of rock fell where I had been standing.

I became a black shadow racing between them, forming thin ropes of smoke that extended from my hands and snaked around the feet of the witches on either side. I reformed my body, then yanked the ropes fast, pulling their feet out from under them. The witches fell face-first toward the ground. I pulled my brother's axe from the holster and brought it down on them one at a time, slicing through their necks with such force, I cracked the stone floor beneath them.

With all four witches dead in a matter of seconds, I fell to my knees in the center of the training room, letting the axe fall from my hand.

Despair and anger surged through me and I let my head fall back as I cried out. Tears fell across my face, freezing before they dropped to the floor and shattered. I wanted revenge. I deserved vengeance.

But more than anything, I wanted my brother back by my side.

WORTH FIGHTING FOR

THE DOOR TO the training room opened and Andros walked through, his blue eyes dark and worried.

I looked away from him, not wanting to see him or hear his excuses right now.

"You don't need to be here right now," I said, reaching for the fallen axe. "I'm not in a mood to be reasoned with."

He didn't leave. Instead, he leaned against the wall by the door, watching me.

"You have grown so much these past few years," he said. "You're a great warrior when you have something in front of you worth fighting for."

I gripped the handle of the axe so tightly my hand hurt from the pressure of it.

"But even a great warrior cannot defeat an entire coven of witches alone," he said. "These witches you killed here were just illusions. They are programmed to fight a certain way, but as long as we don't fully understand the power and magic behind the witches of the Order of Shadows, they are going to remain unpredictable."

"If you came here to talk me out of going after my brother, you can leave right now."

"I came here to let you know that I want to be there by your side when you go after him," he said.

I turned, studying his face. "But Lea said the council decided against going through the portal."

"For now," he said. "But that doesn't mean we can't go in a year or two."

I slung the axe over my shoulder. Of course. He didn't want to stand with me now. He wanted to put off the fight for as long as possible. In a year, he would say we should wait just one more year.

"It will never be enough," I said, my jaw tight. "We will never understand them completely without facing them in battle. It's the only way to know their strengths and discover their weaknesses. And you will never have the courage to fight them."

"I have fought them," he said, moving off the wall to step closer to me. "In the beginning of The Resistance, we all fought them. We did exactly what you're trying to do now. We rushed in, like fools, thinking we could kill them with our anger and rage. I watched some of my best friends die in the blink of an eye. So don't tell me I have no courage."

He rarely spoke of those times when they lost so much.

"Fighting them didn't teach us anything back then," he said. "All we learned was that they cast their magic so fast, we were helpless against them."

"There has to be a way," I said. "We've been studying them for years. We know so much more now than you did back then. We've been training harder. We can defeat them, I know we can."

"You're a fool if you think you can go through that portal and ever come home again," he said.

I swallowed and turned away from him. "What choice do I have?" I asked. "Aerden means everything to me. He's like a part of my own soul. Without him, I don't even know who I am anymore."

"I understand, but—"

"How could you possibly understand?" I asked. "You don't know what it's like to have a twin. It's different from just having a brother. Together, we were stronger."

"I remember," he said, raising an eyebrow.

I narrowed my eyes at him. "What do you mean you remember?" I asked. "You never even met me until Aerden was gone."

He shook his head, the corners of his mouth turning up into a smile. "That's not true," he said. "All this time together and you really don't remember me?"

I lowered the axe, staring at his face.

He shrugged. "I wasn't particularly memorable as a shadowling," he said. "But I remember the two of you. I envied you. When you were together, it was like you could read each other's minds. You played off each other like you were one person, but twice as strong and twice as cunning."

"You knew us as shadowlings?" I asked.

"Yes," he said. "My mother worked in the castle as one of the queen's handmaidens. I grew up right there alongside you and Aerden and the princess. I watched you, mostly, but there were a few times we actually played together."

I shook my head, not remembering him at all. But then, at the edge of my memory, I did remember a boy. Shy and quiet. Always following us around. "There was one boy I remember playing with, but his name was—"

"Dragon," he said, laughing.

My eyes widened. "Yes," I said, remembering now.

He pointed to the red dragon on his armband. "A nickname," he said. "Me, my father, my grandfather. For generations, we have passed down this unique ability to breathe red fire. We are also immune to any type of fire magic. For centuries, our family has been called dragons. When I was a shadowling, my mother called me Dragon because I reminded her so much of my father."

From conversations we'd had in the past, I knew that Andros had lost his father to the Order of Shadows when he was very young. Andros believed he had been taken through an emerald portal near the village of Dumar where he was born.

"I had no idea that was you," I said. "Why didn't you tell me?"

He smiled. "I kind of liked having it as my little secret," he said. "I was so shy as a shadowling, always watching you but never dreaming I could be as strong or have a friend I loved so much. But I do remember how special the bond between you was, even back then. I remember how much he meant to you."

"How can you know that and still expect me to stay?"

Andros moved to stand in front of me. "I don't," he said. "But you can't expect me to come with you when it would put everything I've worked for in danger."

"I have to go," I said.

He put his hand on my shoulder. "I know, my friend. I know."

H closed his eyes, thinking. Finally, he opened tear-filled eyes and nodded. "Okay. I will help you for as long as I can," he said. "Lea, Azira, Ourelia, and I will come with you to the portal. We'll hold it open and clear for you for as long as possible, but we won't go through with you. Denaer, I need for you to understand that if the witches attempt to send anyone through to this side to fight or if the hunter comes back for us, we will go. We will leave you there if we have to."

"I understand." I clapped my hand on his neck and smiled. "Thank you, friend."

Relief flooded through me. They would come with me as far as the portal, but once it was open, I would have to decide to go through on my own. If I was going to save Aerden, that part I would have to do alone.

There was no way to know if I would cross through and ever be able to get home to the shadow world again. All I knew for sure was that I had to try.

I owed my brother that much after all he'd been willing to sacrifice for me.

AT THE MERCY OF TIME

OVER THE NEXT few weeks, I lived on high alert.

We had a plan in place, but in order to get through to the human world, we needed the portal to be opened.

And that meant we needed the Order of Shadows to open it. We knew from watching other portals that sometimes it could be months between rituals, while at some portals the rituals would happen nearly back-to-back. There seemed to be no set time of year or predictable space apart.

So we watched and waited.

We understood from other portal rituals and the books we had taken from the hunter's den that a demon was marked simply by saying their name. Aerden had been different since he was a prima. He had to be there before the ritual even began and he had to be lured out from the king's city. They had needed his power to create the portal.

But for most demons who are taken, all the hunter needs is to have seen them at least once and to know their name. When a ceremony is near and a demon is chosen, the hunter returns to the ring of black roses around the portal. She places a summoning stone inside the ring and chants the name of the chosen demon until the stone begins to glow.

That is how The Resistance has been able to observe so many rituals. Once the hunter has been seen, there are exactly three days before the portal will be opened and the demon will be taken.

I hated to think that we would have to wait for a demon to be taken before we could act against the Order, but there was no other way. We were at the mercy of time.

Someone kept watch on the portal day and night, ready to call us in if there was any activity.

Jericho took the first shift, setting up camp on a hill overlooking the portal. We found the perfect place where he could look down on the portal, but where it would be hard for anyone standing down there to see him or the camp.

He barely slept for days, keeping watch through the night. When Azira came to take his place several days later, he handed her a red communication stone that would allow her to alert us if the hunter appeared. We cycled through several shifts like this, each of us taking a few days at a time.

I grew restless. Lea conjured more and more complex illusions in the training rooms to help me keep my mind off the task ahead, but I lived on the edge, knowing that the call could come at any moment.

When it finally did come, I was in the middle of drawing one of my visions. A new one. I had tossed and turned in my bed for hours before finally getting up and when I switched on the light, a brief vision appeared to me. It was gone as quickly as it had come, and it was only a fraction of a second, but something about it hit me hard.

Something about her.

Because the vision had been so short, I didn't have a clear picture of it in my head. I could only draw out parts of it, but I sat there for a long while, taking care with each detail.

I was standing beneath the window of a large white house, looking up at a human girl. She had long hair and the most beautiful face, but it was her eyes that I remembered. It was her eyes that had pierced through me.

I was drawing this girl when the red communication stone began to glow.

I stopped breathing. My pencil fell from my hand.

This was it. This was the moment that would change my life forever, one way, or another.

The hunter had returned to the portal.

MOMENTS OF BRAVERY

I SAT ON A stone at the edge of the camp, looking down at the large expanse of black rock that led all the way out to the cliffs.

At most we had a few hours before the hunter would return and the portal to the human world would open.

What would I find on the other side?

I closed my eyes and pictured Aerden's face. Was he really still alive? Could these visions of mine really be trusted?

The plan was clear. I would only have a short time to try to find Aerden on the other side of the portal. If I didn't see him or find any answers there, I would have to make a choice. Come home. Or stay.

I stared down at the portal, knowing everything was about to change.

Lea sat down beside me. "You're very brave for going after him."

Was I brave? Or crazy? Maybe there's always a little bit of crazy inside moments of bravery.

"I love him," I said. "I owe him."

She lowered her head. "When Aerden brought me that key, I knew something strange was going on with him," she said. "He'd been acting strange for months. I think the idea of our engagement had him spooked. Maybe he felt that since it had always been the three of us, we were abandoning him by pairing off. I think he felt like he didn't have a place anymore."

I didn't say anything in response. She understood part of what Aerden was feeling, but there was no way she could know the whole truth. I wanted to tell her. If I walked through that portal and didn't return, she would never know she was still loved and that the bright light in that heart stone still shone for her.

But I couldn't tell her. I couldn't find the words to explain it.

After all this time, suddenly, we had none left. There was no time now for all the secret aches and sins we'd kept inside to protect the other's heart.

"Sometimes, I think about the way things might have been if he'd never left," she said. "If he'd never been taken."

I cut my eyes toward her. The suns had long disappeared, but she was beautiful even in darkness. Despite the mask she'd begun to wear all the time to hide her emotions, I still saw her as the girl I'd grown up with. Strong and soft at the same time. Capable of so much love, yet never truly understanding what love was. Would I ever see her again after tonight?

She turned her head slightly and our eyes met. She smiled softly. "It would have been a good life."

I reached for her hand and we sat there together, sharing my last moments in the shadow world in silence, thinking of how things might have been different.

Wondering if they would ever again be the same.

PEACHVILLE

*W*HEN THE TIME came to move down toward the portal, the five of us shifted into shadow and made our way down to the field of black rock. We kept low to the ground, moving slowly in the dark of night.

We got as close as we could to the clearing.

My heart pounded in my chest and I felt as if I couldn't catch my breath. I had waited so long for this moment, and now that it was really here, I had no idea what to expect or how to feel. I think even then, in that moment, I knew it was too much to hope that Aerden would be on the other side to greet me. I knew I wouldn't be coming back with him.

But I had to try. Going through the portal was my destiny.

In the distance, I saw the hunter approaching long before anyone else could. She rose, her decaying form silhouetted against the light of the moons, then flew down toward the clearing.

Yanora. The years had not been kind to her rotting flesh.

The witch on the other side of the portal called out to her, commanding the hunter to give her the name of the demon marked for their dark purpose.

But tonight, there would be more than one demon coming through the portal. Tonight, they would know that the shadow demons were not all like the King of the North. Some of us were willing to risk our lives to fight for those we loved.

My body was tense and ready, my hand closed around the handle of my brother's axe.

I listened as the demon's name was called, the smoky form appearing above the summoning stone, helpless to protest his or her fate. We all breathed a sigh of relief as the hunter, Yanora, was dismissed. She bowed and took her leave.

We knew she would be back as soon as the ritual was disrupted, but her distance would give us time.

On the other side, witches began to chant. I leaned forward, my hands cold as ice.

The familiar blue light pooled on the ground in the center of the roses, then rose, the doorway between our worlds opening. My stomach twisted as the young girl trembled inside the light.

Then, the demon was called forth, summoned through the portal into slavery.

I took a deep breath in and rushed forward with a terrible cry. The blade of my axe sliced through the roses, closing the portal for an instant, but allowing me a brief moment to pass into the circle without being harmed. I pushed through, the roses growing back almost immediately. A terrible heat burned through my left arm just as I pulled it across the circle. I ignored the pain, concentrating only on the job at hand.

I knew I only had a few moments. I had to make every single one count.

As the roses grew back, I saw the others take their places on the outside of the circle of roses, waiting for the hunter. Ready to fight her if that's what it came down to.

Around me, the blue light of the portal rose again, repairing itself and reopening.

I had no time to doubt my choices or hesitate. With all that was left of hope, I charged through the portal, leaving the shadow world and stepping into the ritual room of a small town in Georgia called Peachville.

THE HORROR OF IT ALL

I STEPPED INTO THE ritual room for only a moment before the horror began.

There were more than a dozen witches lined up along the walls of the circular room. Five more stood at the points of a star carved into the stone floor. At the head of the star, near a large blue stone, stood a woman in a blue velvet robe with silver embroidery.

That was all I saw before I was forced into a tight rope of shadowy smoke. I couldn't breathe or control my own body. I heard my axe fall to the floor with a loud clang, my new form unable to hold onto the weapon.

I was pulled with great force toward the body of the teenage girl hovering above the blue light.

I didn't understand it at first, but I couldn't protest or cry out. No matter how hard I struggled, I couldn't regain control. Panic seized me as my smoke snaked around her body, encircling her arms and chest and finally, being pulled straight into her open mouth.

Inside, there was only darkness.

A terrible weight compressed me into a thin ribbon of smoke as the girl inhaled me. The pain of being squeezed so thinly and tightly nearly knocked me unconscious, but I pushed to stay awake. To hold on.

Then, everything stopped.

Everything except the beating of a human heart.

I could hear the blood rushing through her body. I could feel the pull of her magic as she began to siphon my power to make her own stronger.

That's when the horror of it all sank in.

These witches weren't just using demons as slaves and stealing their power through the use of soul stones. They were consuming us. Eating us and forcing us to live inside their bodies without sight or will.

It was unthinkable.

It was evil beyond anything I'd ever known or dreamed.

I would not be held captive inside this girl.

Rage and madness overcame me. I felt the human body surrounding me begin to convulse and shake as I ripped my way through her heart, through her veins, and straight through her chest. Screams rang out through the small ritual room as the girl's lifeless body fell to the floor with a thud.

Two witches rushed forward toward the body and I sent tendrils of smoke toward them, wrapping my power around their throats and squeezing life from them until blood poured from their eyes and mouths.

I knew nothing in those moments but hatred. It tore through my soul the way I'd torn through that poor girl's helpless body. I wanted nothing but destruction and vengeance. I wanted blood.

Every witch who tried to cast a spell my way or flee from the room was brought down by my wrath.

Six witches died, their blood running through the grooves in the five-pointed star, pooling near the blue light of the still-open portal.

And when I turned to face the next witch, the necklace she wore caught the light and I stopped.

Even in my madness, I recognized that necklace. It was a blue pendant on a delicate silver chain and the last time I saw it, it was clutched tightly in my brother's hands and then thrown into a cup of his own blood.

I looked up at the witch. She was not the same girl with braids I had seen on the floor of this room on the day Aerden was taken, but I knew she was the prima. I knew that my brother was enslaved inside her heart, powering her magic.

I pointed my fingers toward the ground, reaching deep inside the earth where I could feel water flowing. I summoned it up through the roots and dirt and through the stone floor of the portal room. I pushed it forward toward the prima and it froze, a river of ice along the floor between us.

I intended to encase her in ice, but the moment the ice touched her foot, a terrible fire broke out along the floor, melting every inch of ice I'd created in the room.

Confused, I cast again, this time pulling daggers of ice from the water and hurling them toward her at impossible speeds. I would kill her if that's what it took.

Only, the ice daggers never reached her.

Instead, a dark shadow formed in front of me. A recreation of the vision I'd had of him. This was the moment I'd been waiting for—dreaming of—for months. And it had turned out to be nothing but a nightmare.

There, in front of me, stood my brother. Half smoke. Half demon.

Protecting the witch who stood behind him.

NOTHING LEFT OF ME TO SAVE

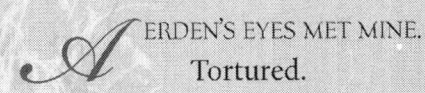

AERDEN'S EYES MET MINE.
 Tortured.
Broken.
Helpless to do anything but protect the prima from harm. He raised his hands against my ice daggers, stopping them from hitting their mark. His fire destroyed my ice.

And I knew that if I lashed out against her again, he would kill me.

Not out of choice.

But out of duty.

He belonged to her now and there was nothing I could do about it.

I stood, stunned. Unable to move or cast or cry. The worst of my nightmares had not even touched the horror of this truth.

In that moment, I wanted to die. I couldn't fight anymore.

On the other side of the portal, Lea screamed my name. I turned my head to see her standing there, bathed in blue light, her hand reaching out toward me. Her eyes panicked.

Behind her, I saw Andros and Ourelia raise their swords against the hunter, Yanora.

I was out of time.

This was the moment I knew would come. The moment where I would have to choose. Stay or go.

I looked into Lea's eyes.

I have to stay. I'm sorry.

"No," she screamed. Her voice was pure desperation. The sound pulled Aerden's attention and he looked to her with such sadness, it broke me in two. She stared at him, then back at me. "No, Denaer. Dammit, come with me. He's gone. You have to let him go, please."

She begged me, tears streaming down her face. I knew I should move quickly, but I couldn't. I was broken from the inside out. There was nothing left of me to save.

I shook my head, then fell to my knees as the witches in the room formed a circle of joined hands. They began to chant and I immediately felt my power start to drain from my body.

Behind her, Andros shouted for Lea to move. He raised his sword against the circle of roses.

Lea clutched her hand to her broken heart, her eyes locked on my face. Andros pulled her back just as the last of the light disappeared and the portal closed.

BORN OF LOVE
THE HUMAN WORLD, PRESENT DAY

I KNELT ON THE ground near the ruined ritual room, the memory stone clutched tightly in my hand.

I had many reasons to hate the Order of Shadows. They had broken my spirit and my heart too many times to count. But the wrath I brought down on those witches the day I came through the portal was every bit as horrible as anything the Order of Shadows has done.

I have hated myself for the darkness that consumed me in those moments.

I lost control. I killed an innocent girl who, before that night, had no idea what it even meant to be initiated into the Order.

But I had paid for my sins. With Harper's help, I had finally put things right here in Peachville. And with her by my side, I wanted to continue this fight against the Order so that every portal could be closed and every human and demon set free.

Would she still love me after she saw the memories I had poured into the stone?

Would she understand why I did what I did? I knew that sharing this with her would either bring us closer together or tear us completely apart.

I could only pray she would forgive me for all the mistakes I had made in my life. I hoped her love was strong enough.

I stood and placed the memory stone in my pocket for the last time tonight. Then, I pulled out the locket Lea had returned to me. My heart stone. It was empty now that she had given it back.

I had never gotten the chance to use this heart stone. Aerden had taken that burden from me, and even though his intentions had been born of love, the lie had caused nothing but pain.

I hoped that someday he would have the courage to tell Lea the truth. But my future happiness was no longer tied to the two of them. My heart belonged to another.

I carefully waved my palm over the delicate golden locket. It fluttered open to reveal an empty stone inside a velvet lining.

I smiled through my tears, then lifted the stone from the case and brought it to my heart.

FINDING LIGHT

I FELT LIKE I could hardly breathe as I walked through the back door of Brighton Manor.

I'd waited my whole life for a night like this, never really believing I would ever get the chance to commit my heart to someone out of choice rather than obligation.

I passed through the halls searching for her. And when I found her, the look in her eyes took my breath away.

She crossed the room and threw her arms around my neck. "Are you done?" she asked.

"Yes," I said, my lips trembling slightly over the word. God, I was as nervous as a shadowling. "I have something I want to show you."

I took her hand in mine and led her through the hall and out the back door.

"Where are you taking me?" Harper asked, giggling as we stepped into the darkness of the forest.

"Hold on," I whispered. I held her tight around the waist, then shifted into smoke and flew us through the trees. I knew that Harper could shift on her own now, too, but it was nice to hold her tight to me, especially after the loneliness of the past few hours.

I stopped just shy of Brighton Lake, taking her human body in my arms and pulling her close to me. "I know it's been a strange night, and I'm sorry I've been so distant," I said, my mouth close to her ear. "But there was something important I needed to do. Something I needed for you to see."

She pulled away so that she could look into my eyes. "What is it?"

I took a deep breath. This was one of the most terrifying moments of my life. I couldn't imagine an eternity without her. In my heart, I knew she wouldn't turn her back on me. But at the same time, showing someone your deepest, darkest moments was never easy. It's so rare that you love someone enough to really bare your soul to them like that.

Or maybe it was trust that was rare.

"It comes in two parts," I said. I took the quartz stone from my pocket. "This is called a memory stone. It allows you to see and feel any memory that has been placed inside of it. I have spent most of my night in the past, remembering everything that happened from the time Aerden was first taken all the way until the day I came here to try to save him."

I took Harper's hand and opened her palm, then placed the stone inside.

"When you close your fist around the stone and close your eyes, you'll be able to see everything I experienced during that time in my life," I said. "There are so many things you don't know about me. Things that happened to me. Things I have done. And even the things you do know, like what I did when I came through the portal, you might not truly understand. I know I have kept so many secrets from you in the past, but I don't want there to be any more secrets. I want you to understand everything about me, even the horrible things I have done in my life."

She stared at the stone in her hand, then looked up, her eyes meeting mine. "Jackson, I love you no matter what you've done," she said. "I love for you everything that you are, even the darkest parts of you that you haven't wanted anyone to see."

I ran the back of my fingers across the softness of her cheek. "I don't deserve you," I said in a whisper.

"I wish you could see yourself the way I do," she said. "There is no one in this world or the next who deserves love and happiness more than you. And no matter what I see inside these memories, there's nothing that will ever take away from the love I feel for you. I hope you know that."

"We're going to face some tough times ahead," I said, thinking of what I knew we would soon have to face. "The peace we've known the last few months isn't going to last. I needed to show you these memories in order to let go of the past. It's the only way we're going to move forward."

Harper nodded, then sat down on a fallen log. She took a deep breath, closed her eyes, then slowly closed her fist around the stone.

She sat still and quiet for a long time as the memories flowed through her. I knew it wasn't exactly like watching a movie or seeing these things happen in real time. It was more of an absorbing of knowledge. Fifty years of my life were flowing through her mind in the span of only an hour. It would be a lot for her to take in.

I paced the path in front of her, waiting.

When she finally opened her eyes, tears cascaded down her cheeks.

I held my breath, not knowing what to expect.

She stood up slowly, walked toward me, then placed her palm against my face. She looked deep into my eyes and my heart raced.

"You are the most loving, most loyal, most beautiful being I have ever known," she said. Her voice hitched on the words.

"Everything you have ever done has been born of love. I'm the one who doesn't deserve you."

Hearing those words from her was like finding light in the darkest corners of my heart. I slid my hands around her waist and lifted her, holding her tightly against my body. She wrapped her arms around my neck and lifted her lips to mine.

I poured my love into that kiss. My gratefulness. All the ache of the past melted away in those moments as her lips touched mine. I breathed her in and held her close, never wanting to let her go.

But there was one more thing I needed to do tonight.

One more secret hope in my heart.

When we parted, she smiled, her eyes twinkling. "What's the second part?"

"The second part is more fun," I said, taking her hand. "Close your eyes."

She closed her eyes and let me lead her the rest of the way down the path toward Brighton Lake. When we got to the small dock surrounded by white roses, I smiled and nervously told her to open her eyes.

She opened them slowly, then gasped, fresh tears springing to her eyes.

Along the dock and floating across the entire lake were more than a thousand white candles.

"You did all this for me?" she asked.

"This is only the beginning of what I hope to someday do for you."

I reached into my pocket and pulled out two items. A small piece of paper and a golden locket.

I unfolded the worn paper. It was fifty years old and had been folded and unfolded a lot during that time. There wasn't much to the drawing itself. I'd never really had a chance to finish it.

"I drew this just before I came through the portal to Peachville," I said. "I had stuffed it in my pocket at the time, not really understanding its significance. In the days following the ritual, when I was broken and powerless, bound to human form and thrown in the attic at Shadowford, I spent a lot of time looking at this drawing, wondering how my future would ever lead me to something so beautiful."

I handed her the drawing.

It was simple, but clear. A girl with long blond hair and brown eyes standing in a window looking down at a boy, seeing him for the first time. Neither of them understanding exactly how much they would mean to each other.

"The moment I looked up at that window and saw these eyes staring back at me, I knew that everything in my life had been leading me to you."

I took her hand in mine, then slowly dipped to one knee before her.

"I know it's human custom to give a woman a ring when you propose to her, but in the demon culture we share heart stones to reveal our true intentions. Our deepest feelings. From my memories, you know that I never got to use my heart stone with Lea. My engagement to her was never real, no matter what anyone else may have thought. I never chose her. And I never loved her the way I love you."

Her lips parted slightly and her hand trembled in mine.

"Harper Madison Brighton, never in almost two hundred years of life did I ever dream I could find a love like this. You are the strongest, bravest, most amazing woman I have ever known." Tears of love and joy streamed down my face as I looked up into the eyes of the woman I loved. "Every moment of pain and heartache. Every broken piece of my soul. It was all worth it because it was all leading me here to this moment, with you. You have made me whole again. You have brought me happiness when I thought there was no hope. If you'll have me, I want to spend the rest of my life with you."

She took the golden locket in her shaking hands, then fell to her knees on the ground in front of me.

"I have no life without you," she said.

She leaned into me, her body warm and quivering against mine. I kissed her there among her mother's beloved white roses. The place where she and her sister had spread their father's ashes.

The place where we'd had our first date.

Where our two worlds opened up to each other. Not from the evil magic of a corrupted witch's greed for power, but from the love between a demon king and a human girl.

This was the way our two worlds deserved to be joined. This was the way it was in the beginning and the way it was always meant to be. We would make it right again, even if it took a hundred lifetimes.

"Are you going to open it?" I asked her between kisses, motioning to the locket that still held the heart stone.

"Yes," she said, smiling through her tears.

She set the locket against her palm, then waved her hand across the top of it.

I pulled her close as the locket opened, revealing a light so bright and a love so strong, a thousand candles could never compare.

A light we would both cling to in the dark days to come.

ABOUT SARRA—

Sarra Cannon writes contemporary and paranormal fiction with both teen and college aged characters. Her novels often stem from her own experiences growing up in the small town of Hawkinsville, Georgia, where she learned that being popular always comes at a price and relationships are rarely as simple as they seem.

She has sold over a quarter of a million books since she first began her career as an Indie author in 2010.

Sarra is a devoted (obsessed) fan of Hello Kitty and has an extensive collection that decorates her desk as she writes. She currently lives in South Carolina with her amazingly supportive husband and her adorable son.

Connect with Sarra online!
Website: SarraCannon.com
Facebook: Facebook.com/sarracannon
Instagram: instagram.com/sarracannon
Twitter: twitter.com/sarramaria
Goodreads: Goodreads.com/Sarra_Cannon

Made in the USA
Lexington, KY
24 December 2015